FIC
Smi

Homemade
Humble
Pie

Other books by Annette Smith

*The Whispers of Angels*
*Stories to Feed Your Soul*
*Help! My Little Girl's Growing Up*

# Homemade Humble Pie

## and Other Slices of Life

Stories by

## Annette Smith

Fleming H. Revell

A Division of Baker Book House Co
Grand Rapids, Michigan 49516

© 2001 by Annette Smith

Published by Fleming H. Revell
a division of Baker Book House Company
P.O. Box 6287, Grand Rapids, MI 49516-6287

Printed in the United States of America

**Library of Congress Cataloging-in-Publication Data**

Smith, Annette Gail, 1959–
    Homemade humble pie : and other slices of life : stories / by Annette Smith.
        p.    cm.
    ISBN 0-8007-5771-8
    1. Southern States—Social life and customs—Fiction. 2. Humorous stories, American.  I. Title.
    PS 3619.M55 H66    2001
    813'.6—dc21                                                    2001041624

Unless otherwise indicated, Scripture is taken from the HOLY BIBLE, NEW INTERNATIONAL VERSION®. NIV®. Copyright © 1973, 1978, 1984 by International Bible Society. Used by permission of Zondervan Publishing House. All rights reserved.

Scripture marked KJV is taken from the King James Version of the Bible.

Scripture marked TLB is taken from The Living Bible © 1971. Used by permission of Tyndale House Publishers, Inc., Wheaton, IL 60189. All rights reserved.

For current information about all releases from Baker Book House, visit our web site:
http://www.bakerbooks.com

For Dad

# *Contents*

# Acknowledgments

Many thanks to the following folks:

Randy, my husband of twenty-two years, who is forever my cheerleader, my champion, my friend.

Russell and Rachel, kids who, as they've moved from childhood to young adulthood, have become two of the people with whom I most enjoy spending time.

Louie and Marolyn Woodall, my parents, who continually inspire me with their curiosity, their zest for life, their willingness to adapt, grow, and change.

Sheila Cook, my friend who, although she isn't "in the business," takes an affirming interest in all that I do. Not even once have I seen her eyes glaze over when I describe in verbose detail what it is I plan to write about next!

Chip MacGregor, my agent and friend, whose guidance and wisdom enable my career.

The good folks at Revell, for all they've done to transform my humble words into this lovely book.

*To God be the glory!*

# Introduction

My mother is a terrific Southern cook. In the house where I grew up, marvelous smells wafted from the kitchen, down the hall, and into my bedroom. All I had to do was take a good sniff and I could tell what was for supper that night.

My dad has an insatiable sweet tooth, and so the finale of almost every meal my mother prepared was a fresh-from-the-oven dessert. Although she made great cakes and cookies, pies were her specialty. The sight of her working a rolling pin over a flour-covered board would get my younger twin brothers so excited at the prospect of pie that they'd march around the kitchen clapping and singing "Crust and Obey," their unique version of a well-known hymn.

Everyone I know likes to eat pie—and why not? There's homespun calm and comfort to be found in a sliver of tender crust that's been filled with something sweet. Following a meal or eaten as a snack, consumed with a glass of cold milk or a cup of steaming coffee, pie's sure to warm both body and soul.

The ingredients called for in most any kind of pie are deceptively simple—sugar, salt, flour, nuts, fruit, or cream. Nothing fancy, yet oh-so-good.

Likewise, both the fictional and the true slice-of-life stories in this book capture the simplest of life's experiences—love and laughter, faith and family, hopes and dreams. What could be better? Sweeter? Of greater value? It is my hope that you, dear reader, will savor these gentle stories in much the same way that you enjoy a piece of pie. Sink into a comfy chair; prop your feet up on something soft. Take your time and savor every bite, for I've prepared dessert—especially for you!

Part 1

*And the Two
Shall Become One*

ONE

# Class Reunion

Mock potato salad.
Asparagus guacamole.
Fat-free french fries.

It happens every spring. The ranks of the Shadow Rock Tuesday-night Weight Watchers class swell to their annual high when invitations to the twenty-year class reunion begin arriving in mailboxes all over town.

The year 1997 was no exception. By the time the two-months-to-reunion countdown had begun, so many new members had signed up for the calorie-counting class that an unprecedented move was made from the cramped United Methodist's young adult Sunday school classroom to the newly carpeted fellowship hall at First Baptist just down the street. Paying rapt attention to the class leader, the portly, thirty-something members of the class of '77 scribbled notes, copied recipes word-for-word, and prayed for nothing less than a metabolic miracle.

Weight Watchers wasn't the only part of the town's economy that reaped financial rewards thanks to the reunion. Sam Sheety, owner and pharmacist at Sam's Drugstore, lost track of how many Retin-A prescriptions he filled. His store shelves were completely cleaned out of tooth whitening products, men's hair color, and self-tanning creams. Tawny Banks, owner and operator of Shadow Rock's beauty salon, Tawny's Unisex Beauty Bar, advertised a special on foil highlights and offered two-for-one lip and eyebrow waxings. She found herself happily busy the entire week preceding the reunion. Mort Hammers' Shady Hollow Motel was completely booked. Not even one of his fourteen air-conditioned rooms remained unreserved.

According to the class secretary, Faith Ann Harling, the official list revealed that fifty-two out of sixty-five graduates were coming. Linda and Ed Jenkins. Marcie and John Hollinsworth. Elizabeth and Stanley Crudd. Even Elaine and Mark Giddings were expected. News was, the popular high-school couple (former marching band sweetheart and state 4-H winter grass judging champion) had bought discount airplane tickets six months ago and would be flying from wherever it was they lived now. . . . Missouri or Minnesota . . . *one* of those faraway, M-sounding states . . . Montana, maybe. (Geography was not Faith Ann's best subject in school.)

Another out-of-towner, Tara Ticker, returned her registration form well before the deadline. Sent it overnight mail, in fact. Tara had not been expected to come—what with her five divorces and all. Bless her heart. That many unhappy husbands would have to be a bit embarrassing for anyone. That was the consensus at the reunion committee meeting, anyway.

"Such a shame," declared committee chairperson Janice Banks, shaking her head at the mention of Tara's multiple, misguided, marital matches.

Committee members nodded their sympathetic agreement, vying for a nonchalant peek at Tara's completed registration form. Would a five-time divorcée dare to show up with a date? Yes ma'am, she would. Right there, on the bottom right-hand corner of her registration form, in red ink, Tara had checked the box affirming "guest attending."

If nothing else, Tara was an optimistic girl.

As the day of the big evening approached, the five-person reunion committee congratulated itself on months of hard work. They had devoted a ton of effort—searching phone books, calling parents for classmates' whereabouts, addressing and licking endless legal-sized envelopes—to make this a festive event, and they couldn't wait to enjoy the fruits of their labor. Lord willing, on July 23, the graduating class of 1977 would gather in the recently remodeled VFW hall to fellowship with one another and feast on barbecued beef brisket and white bread, slow-cooked pinto beans, coleslaw and sliced onions, chocolate sheet cake, iced tea, and coffee.

Such pride did the committee take in planning the event that they would have been shocked and hurt to know that not everyone on the guest list shared their anticipation.

For although she politely kept it to herself, my friend Denise was one such ungrateful soul.

Truth be told, although seven and three-quarter pounds lighter since the first of April, Denise was not exactly looking forward to the reunion. Having knowingly let the May 1 deadline pass without sending in her reservation form, it had been a struggle, Denise confided to me, to feign appropriate gratitude when Faith Ann called and graciously assured her that she was in luck—it was not yet too late to sign up. Faith Ann would even stop by the house to pick up Denise's registration form herself.

"You don't need to do that," Denise protested. "That's entirely too much trouble."

"It is not! Just leave your form in the mailbox and I'll pick it up on my way to work. Won't be out of my way at all. A reunion is not something to be missed!" Faith Ann asserted.

Denise's husband, Darrell, watched his wife squirm. "How come you don't want to go?" he asked.

"Don't you want to see your old friends, Mom?" her eighteen-year-old daughter, Amber, questioned.

Denise didn't answer but instead concentrated on making coffee and spreading butter on Darrell's toast, diet margarine on her own. *Lots of my old girlfriends will be there,* she mused. *Sarah and Celina, Wendy and Lace. But what in the world will we find to talk about after all this time? And what about Andy? What if he comes?*

Denise and I have been friends forever. We went to grade school together, then high school, and even took nurse's training at the same time. We work the same shifts during the week, sit beside each other at Friday-night basketball games, and spend our Sunday mornings standing side by side in the choir loft at First Community Church.

I knew why she was skittish about attending the reunion—she had not seen Andy Harmon in twenty years. Andy was Denise's first love. There had been no doubt in her mind, or in any of her friends' minds, that he was the one for her. Granted, they had made an odd couple—Andy a cigarette-smoking, wild boy from the wrong side of town; Denise a quiet, obedient, churchgoing girl. None of us could figure out what they saw in each other—but did they ever have it bad! Her parents reluctantly let them date (Friday nights only; home by eleven), and Andy did his best to clean up his act. He quit smoking and went to school almost every day. Denise was so proud of him. The two of them made secret plans to be together forever, speaking over the phone in late-night whispers about getting married someday and having a cute little house and cute little children.

But to everyone's shock, it never happened. On graduation day, with no warning or explanation, Andy's best friend delivered the stunning message: Andy wanted to break up.

And so they did. Just like that. Denise was left feeling dizzy and disoriented, wondering what it was she had done that was so terribly wrong. The week after graduation she looked for him in town, jumped whenever the phone rang, imagined she saw his car in the driveway. Only when she learned that he'd moved three states away did Denise stop all that looking.

"I don't know," Denise finally answered Amber and Darrell. "Reunions are never all they're cracked up to be. I'm not sure I want to go. I may have to work that night anyway."

Later as she studied herself in the bathroom mirror, thinking about the reunion, Denise concluded that she had let herself go. Over the years she'd gained weight—most of it through her hips. Her hair and complexion looked dull and she didn't have one decent dress in her whole closet.

And what in her life would impress anyone? Although she had been valedictorian and voted "Most Likely to Succeed," she had not gone to the university she had planned on. Instead she had put Andy out of her mind and married Darrell, vice president of his church's youth group, the fall after graduation. She'd given birth to Amber nine months later and spent the next ten years keeping house. Amber was in first grade before Denise had even gone to community college, and then not to study medicine, or law, or even accounting, but practical nursing. And although she liked it all right, a job at Happy Acres Rest Home was not exactly cause to brag.

19

However, due in great part to Faith Ann's persistence, Denise shed a few pounds, trimmed her bangs, and bought herself a new black dress—soft wool crepe, trimmed in a deep shade of red. The night of the reunion, after she had stepped into stockings, pulled on the dress, and dabbed on lipstick, Denise looked in the mirror and acknowledged that this was the best she could do.

"You look real nice, honey," Darrell told her.

"Pretty dress, Mom," Amber offered.

But Denise knew she didn't look one bit like she did back then.

Neither did any of the rest of us, and I think we were all greatly relieved. Classmates had gained weight. Some had lost hair, and some had grown hair in places where hair is not celebrated. Chins, arms, and bellies of formerly perky cheerleaders now sagged, and a couple of ex-football players conversed with red faces, struggling mightily to hold their middle-aged middles in check.

A few of our class members bragged of their great successes. Most did not. Nearly everyone had kids, and a handful even had grandchildren.

As we conversed in the ladies' room, Denise and I agreed that the reunion was not turning out to be as uncomfortable as we'd feared. Our out-of-town friends Sarah, Celina, Wendy, and Lace were there, accompanied by what we deemed to be fairly pleasant husbands. After only a few awkward moments, the six of us became comfortable. And so we laughed and we talked and we even planned to get together again soon.

It was after the barbecue and the announcements when Denise, on her way to the ladies' room, saw forty-year-old Andy (he'd failed two grades) sitting against the shadowy back wall, almost hidden by the hired disc jockey's elaborate electrical setup. Looking stiff in a sport coat and tie, he was sipping a beer and talking quietly with some of his old buddies.

Once she'd spotted him, Denise had trouble concentrating on Darrell and the rest of us. It was embarrassing for her, although I suspect I was the only one who noticed. No matter how hard she tried to control them, Denise's eyes keep flitting back to the corner where Andy was sitting. When he glanced toward our table, her face flushed a bit and she took a couple of deep breaths.

*What is that all about?* Denise chided herself. *It has been twenty years. You are a grown woman.* When Darrell went to get her a second Diet Coke, Denise opened the souvenir reunion booklet prepared by the committee and read about Andy. Unemployed and divorced times two. Address? A post office box in a town across state. Hobbies? Racing cars, playing pool.

Darrell returned. "Having a good time?" She smiled at him and scooted her chair a bit closer to his, resting her hand on his knee.

A couple of hours passed. Except to get more beer, Andy didn't move from his spot, never attempted to mingle with any of us or even to speak to anyone except the guys at his table. Denise was both relieved and strangely disappointed that he didn't say hello. *Truth is, he probably doesn't even recognize me.*

It was not until the reunion was over and she and Darrell were starting toward the door that Andy rose from his seat. He left his corner and stepped quickly across the hall to stand before her and Darrell. He *had* seen her, known she was there all along, and just waited until now to speak.

Denise drew a breath. Said, "Hello, nice to see you." Took note of her hips and sucked her stomach in. Andy barely glanced at Denise, but instead thrust out his hand to shake Darrell's.

"Andy Harmon," he said.

"Pleased to meet you. Darrell Tucker."

Andy swallowed and looked Darrell straight in the eye. "I just want you to know that you got yourself a good woman.

A real good woman. The worst mistake I ever made in my life was letting her get away."

Darrell, caught off guard and clueless as to who this man might be, simply returned the shake and said, "Thank you. Thank you very much."

On the way home, Darrell didn't mention the unexpected exchange; in fact, he seemed to think nothing of it. Denise was surprised. Surely he would be curious. Perhaps a little bit jealous? But he didn't seem to be. He kept his eyes on the road, wondered aloud if Amber had remembered to feed the cat, spoke about plans for the weekend and how much he dreaded tomorrow's appointment with the dentist.

Denise struggled to pay attention to the conversation, but it was difficult because Andy's words resounded in her head. She heard them over and over while they were in the car. They echoed in her ear while she locked the doors, while she peeked in on Amber, while she dressed for bed. They continued to sound as she lay in the bed, curled next to Darrell. Even as she drew close to sleep she heard, *You got yourself a good woman. . . . Worst mistake I ever made in my life was letting her get away.*

Gently, Darrell's arms eased around her. A moment passed. Finally he whispered in her neck, "You know that guy?"

"Hmmm?" she murmured.

"The one at the reunion."

Denise held her breath.

"He was right you know," Darrell finished with a catch in his voice.

And so slowly, a fully awake Denise turned in the bed to face her husband. Placing first a gentle, then a not-so-gentle kiss on his lips, she acknowledged that Faith Ann Harling had been right all along.

A reunion is not something to be missed.

*A wife of noble character who can find?*
  *She is worth far more than rubies.*
*Her husband has full confidence in her*
  *and lacks nothing of value.*
*She brings him good, not harm,*
  *all the days of her life.*

PROVERBS 31:10–12

# Music for Two

Eighty-year-old Winnie went to work. Husband Weldon, seventy-seven years old, stayed at home. Though unusual, their occupational arrangement suited the couple just fine.

A car wreck years ago left Weldon weak and unable to stand for long periods of time, but he managed to keep the house with marvelous efficiency. Moving at a slow but steady pace, he cheerfully did the laundry and the dusting. The cooking he truly enjoyed, especially the baking. Twice a week, Weldon made several loaves of bread, preparing them in one-pound coffee cans with a decades-old recipe gleaned from "Hints from Heloise."

Winnie, although well past the time when most folks retire, allowed only one concession to her age. When she turned seventy, she cut back her work week from five and a half to four days a week. Every Monday through Thursday Winnie worked at her desk inside Crabtree's Fine New and Used Furniture, her place of employment for the past thirty-seven years. Winnie enjoyed her bookkeeping job—keeping records, tending to accounts receivable and payable, writing checks—even if she didn't particularly care for young John Crabtree, who had never learned to do things with the efficiency of his father, John Crabtree Sr. (God rest his soul.)

Personal feelings aside, Winnie treated young John with all the honor and respect an eighty-year-old woman can reasonably be expected to muster for a man twenty years her junior. As a result she and young John got along fine for the most part. Only when Winnie occasionally decided to award herself a healthy pay raise would a red-faced young John, ledger clutched in his shaking hand, step into her office and ask for an explanation. Each time the young man got himself worked up like that, Winnie felt pity and willingly agreed that from now on she would certainly discuss such matters first. (Since she only gave herself a raise when she truly deserved it, Winnie secretly wondered at all the fuss.) Then to prove proper penance, Winnie would grandly and graciously offer to resign if her work was deemed unsatisfactory.

Each time she did so, young John, honoring the words his late father had extorted from him (that he would not sell the furniture store and that he would never get rid of Miz Winnie; she has that sick husband, you know), would shake his head, mop nervous sweat from his brow, and assure Winnie, yet again, that her work was just fine.

It didn't seem natural for a woman to work and a man to keep house, and through the years many in the small town gossiped about how Winnie wore the pants in the family. Truth be told, with her husband being in the shape he was, Winnie did have to take charge of a lot of things she would have just as soon let Weldon do. But he simply wasn't able, so they seldom spoke of such things.

The last time Weldon could remember their sharing anything even close to sharp words was when during supper one night, around the beginning of the fourth decade of their union, he innocently wondered aloud why all of a sudden he was going through so many pairs of undershorts. Seemed like every time he turned around he was washing a load. He wasn't changing his clothes any more often and hadn't let the laundry pile up. At least he didn't *think* he had. Weldon scratched his head.

Winnie chewed her buttered bread, swallowed, and tried to change the subject. Had Weldon put extra cinnamon in the bread this time? Tasted like it. Nutmeg perhaps?

Never a man to be easily distracted, Weldon told her no, and what about this laundry quandary?

Feeling forced, Winnie told all. A while back she had taken to wearing Weldon's underwear instead of her own. His boxers, she discovered, were a lot more comfortable than her own fitted underpants, which suddenly had begun to bother her to no end. His drawers, she found, fit better, didn't bind or ride up in back, and didn't chafe. They seemed to wear better, too. Was this a problem for Weldon?

Well, no, now that you mention it. Just took a bit of getting used to is all. Actually, the thought of his slim wife, buttoned into her beige-and-brown workday shirtwaist, wearing his paisley-print shorts underneath her slip, was for Weldon a rather stirring one.

Although Winnie and Weldon lived very different lives, they had a special bond that brought them together. After supper each night they spent a couple of quiet hours reclined side by side in matching La-Z-Boys, watching reruns of *The Lawrence Welk Show* on cable television. They were both big-band music fans, Winnie especially, and the music always ended too soon to suit her, with Mr. Welk's band not playing a certain song she wanted to hear. Weldon suggested they purchase some big-band recordings so they could listen to any song they wanted, whenever they wanted, but Winnie didn't think so.

It didn't seem practical to buy a whole record just to get one or two songs.

Winnie and Weldon's life had developed a comfortable routine since Weldon's accident and Winnie's joining the workforce. But one day, this routine began to change. Weldon was not a worrier by nature, but one early spring evening Winnie didn't come home on time. When she was more than an hour late, he got anxious and called a neighbor to help him look for her. They found her at the gas station where she always filled up, holding the gas pump in her hand, confused, unable to figure out what came next. Weldon thought she must be sick, likely coming down with an early summer flu.

Once they got home, Winnie was fine. She ate a hearty supper, seemed to have enjoyed a good day at work, and did not want to talk about what had happened at the station. Weldon let it go, but he watched her closely all night, examined her eyes in the morning before she set out to work, and phoned young John Crabtree to ask him to keep an eye on Winnie and call him if she seemed ill.

John didn't call that day and everything seemed fine. But it wasn't; at least not for much longer.

Within months Winnie became so forgetful that she had to stop working. Weldon convinced himself that the job was just too much for a woman her age. He should have insisted she retire years ago. Once she got home and rested up she would be just fine.

But she wasn't. Winnie put birdseed in the dog's bowl, dog food in the bird feeder, and a stick of butter in her purse. She left the water running all night in the bathroom sink and planted microwave popcorn in the potted ivy. She put Weldon's blood-pressure medicine in the freezer and her false teeth in the dirty clothes hamper. Even though they didn't own a VCR, she sent off for a bunch of videotapes from one of those clubs.

Weldon was beside himself, worn out, and sick at heart. When Winnie began falling almost everyday, choking on her food, and going through so many pairs of underwear that he couldn't keep up, he gave in to several months of nudgings from his wife's doctor.

Two days after Thanksgiving, Weldon put Winnie, his wife of fifty-four years, in a nursing home.

And, oh, how he hated it.

From the day Winnie was admitted, Weldon nearly drove me and the other nurses crazy with his faultfinding. Winnie's bed wasn't made right. Winnie's clothing wasn't washed properly. Winnie didn't eat beans cooked like that. Winnie took her medicine with apple juice, not grape. No matter how hard we tried to please the man, no matter how much extra attention we gave his wife, nothing satisfied him. I doubted that anything we did ever would.

Adding to the poor man's brokenhearted misery was the fact that Winnie seemed to love everything about the nursing home. On the days she was alert, she pointed out the nice features of the home to Weldon. "Look at those pretty curtains," I heard her say to him. "Isn't that little nurse sweet?" she confided. "I've never had such delicious pecan pie," she exclaimed. Refusing to be swayed, Weldon countered each of Winnie's positive comments with a negative statement of his own.

Until the day he heard the music.

I was dispensing medications from a rolling cart just outside Winnie's door. That night Weldon had cooked at home and then brought the supper to the nursing home. The two of them had eaten together, not in the noisy communal dining room, but wedged knee-to-knee on Winnie's bed, their meal spread out on the over-bed table. Weldon had brought chicken pie, peas, and dessert. I watched as he spooned Winnie a last bite of pudding, then gently wiped her face and hands.

"Weldon . . ." Winnie spoke in a dreamy voice.

"What is it, dear?"

"Don't you just love the sound of that band?"

"Band?"

"You know, the one they have here at this place."

Weldon's face fell. His wife had been alert during supper, almost herself.

"Oh, Weldon, I just love listening to that band. It plays all the time." She smiled.

"You hear a band? All the time?" Weldon questioned.

"Oh, yes. And the best thing about the band they have here is that it will play any song you want to hear, any time you want to hear it. They are wonderful musicians. Listen real close. You'll be able to hear them, too."

From my place at the door, I watched Weldon. At first he hesitated, then he took Winnie's hand and looked her in the eyes.

"Hear them?" She waited expectantly for Weldon's response. Seconds passed. Finally, he nodded.

"Aren't they good?"

She waited again. And after a long moment, Weldon smiled at his wife and gave her a gentle peck on her wrinkled pink cheek. "Yes," he said. "They're very good."

Winnie grinned, leaned her head on his shoulder, and then as if of their own accord, her toes began to tap.

A moment later I saw Weldon's toes begin to tap, too.

And as I moved to my next resident's room, I smiled, for I found that I as well—at least for tonight—stepped in time to the music that Winnie could hear.

> *Where morning dawns and evening fades*
> *you call forth songs of joy.*
>
> PSALM 65:8

# THREE

# Electric-Blanket Bliss

Tasha West, a ten-year-old so skinny that during games of Red Rover she was always the first called to come over, found herself embroiled in a disturbing grade-school scandal. It was easy to trace the whole mess to a specific noontime when, hunched over Salisbury steaks and canned peaches, Tasha swore her seven best friends to utter secrecy before confessing to them who it was she liked.

"Swear you won't tell?"

"We swear."

"On your great-aunts' graves?"

"On our great-aunts' graves."

(Of the seven, only Tasha's third best friend, Marcie Maldin, refused to swear. Marcie's mother told her swearing was a sin, sort of like cussing, and besides, she didn't *have* a great-aunt. Tasha made a hasty exception and agreed to let Marcie get by on a promise instead of a swear.)

"Come on, Tasha. Who is it? We won't tell."

"Joe Pringle."

"No way!" They were shocked and embarrassed for their friend. "Joe Pringle? A first grader? He hasn't even lost a tooth yet. He's short. He's *two years* younger than us. Tasha, a third grader can't like a first grader."

But Tasha did. And the word spread like wildfire. By 3:00 that afternoon everyone from kindergarten to fifth grade had heard the news. The shock and disapproval were universal.

"Cradle robber!"

"Baby-sitter!"

"Whatsa matter, can't get a boy your own age?"

Tasha didn't care. Although she was mad at Marcie (obviously the unsworn source of the leak), she would not be swayed from her devotion to the cutest boy in school.

And Joe Pringle? Basking in unexpected, unearned, *glorious,* first-grade notoriety, he was thrilled to death. A six-year-old man of action, Joe came right out and asked his best friend to ask Tasha's best friend if Tasha would go with him.

The May-December romance blossomed during long school-bus rides, next-to-each-other seats at school assemblies, and forbidden school-night phone calls.

Ten years later, with a six-month-layaway diamond ring from Wal-Mart, it was Joe's turn to create scandal.

"Engaged?" His friends couldn't believe it. "Man, you're only sixteen. You don't even have a car yet. Besides, Tasha's already eighteen. Isn't she going to college next year? You've gotta be crazy, Joe!"

"Engaged?" his parents thundered. "What about your education? What about football? What about the fact that you can't even remember to take out the trash on Fridays? You're too young to even think about getting married!"

But getting married to Tasha was all Joe could think about. After all, he'd dreamed about marrying Tasha since the day she got the ball rolling.

But the two of them did wait—right up until the first Saturday night after Joe's graduation from high school and Tasha's commencement from community college. Tasha had finished up X-ray school in two years and had landed a job in the radiology department at the hospital. The plan was for her to work and Joe to attend school.

The wedding was a big production. The church was lavishly adorned with silk flowers, scented candles, and dozens of iridescent butterflies carefully crafted of lavender tulle.

Tasha appeared beaming and beautiful in a fluffy, puffy, Cinderella-style gown; the only fairy-tale paraphernalia missing were glass slippers, ugly stepsisters, and a pumpkin-patch transport. Joe stood before his family and friends, happy but itchy in a too-tight, funny-smelling, rented tuxedo, eager to get the show on the road.

The honeymoon, paid for with Joe's graduation money, amounted to three days and two nights at a deluxe Holiday Inn thirty miles down the road. The free breakfast buffet at the hotel, lunch at McDonald's, dinner at El Chico, and movies at the dollar movie theater gave them many good memories. They were blissfully, wonderfully, perfectly together at last.

But when they returned from their honeymoon, reality set in. They were both only children and unaccustomed to compromise, so they fought all the time, usually about stupid stuff like tuna-fish salad and paying bills.

Joe's mama made tuna fish with Miracle Whip, tart apples, and lots of chopped nuts. Tasha insisted on making tuna fish like her mother did, with real mayonnaise, sweet red onions, and spoonfuls of pickle relish.

Joe said onions made Tasha's breath stink. Tasha said too bad. If Joe didn't like the way her breath smelled, then he wouldn't be wanting to get close enough to sniff it, would he? Which, by the way, was fine by her.

And then there were the bills.

Tasha believed all responsible adults took the bills from the mailbox, carried them directly into the house, laid them on the kitchen table, opened them, wrote checks for them, stuffed the envelopes, sealed and stamped them, and put them right back into the mailbox. Not the same week, not the same day, but preferably the same hour as their arrival. Anything less timely than that made her nervous. After all, they couldn't afford to be casual about their credit rating, now could they?

Joe, however, didn't seem as concerned about their credit. When he retrieved the mail, the bills got casually tossed onto a chair or into a drawer. Which drawer? Any drawer. He didn't pay much attention. After all, the bills didn't need to be paid for a month or so. What was the fuss?

Many times Tasha, searching for a cookie coupon or a Phillips screwdriver, would come across an unopened bill from the electric company or from the cable TV people. Frightened and upset, she'd scream like she'd seen a snake or something. Joe would dash to her side, fully prepared to lend masculine aid, only to find his bride red-faced with anger. At him.

Finally, Tasha told Joe to just let her bring in the mail from now on. She would keep things sorted out, since he obviously wasn't up to the task. Which of course made him eager to beat her to the mailbox every day.

Things were most interesting if they were both home during the day. When the mail arrived (they'd be steely-eyed, watching for the man all morning long), the front door of their tiny house would fly open, and Tasha and Joe would sprint to the mailbox, each determined to get there first. If a tie occurred, a heated shoving match was the result, with bills and flyers and letters scattering across the yard and into the street.

The curious contest provided sidesplitting entertainment for their next-door neighbors who had been married for fifty-two years. Enjoying cups of coffee on the front porch, the couple watched and chuckled and made predictions on who would claim the prize that day, Tasha or Joe.

It was generally a fifty-fifty split.

When Joe and Tasha got engaged, they picked out china and flatware, towels and sheets. However, I wanted to get them something that they likely wouldn't think of themselves, something not on their list. My husband and I have slept under an electric blanket for years, and we agree that nothing compares to crawling into an already-warm bed on a chilly winter evening and staying warm throughout the night. What better gift for a young couple just starting out, living in a drafty house and trying to save on natural gas, than an electric blanket? I bought a lovely rose-colored one on sale, wrapped it up, and presented it to them at the bridal shower given by the church.

How was I to know that my carefully chosen present would be the source of more marital strife?

Tasha loved the blanket. It provided the warmth her slender, shivering body craved, and for the first time in her life, she could sleep all night without getting cold. Even her toes stayed toasty.

Joe liked the blanket, too. Even after a day of discord, the two of them could count on snuggling the night away in electric-blanketed bliss.

Until Joe, randomly flipping through TV channels one afternoon, came upon a convincing tabloid news story about how low-voltage electricity could give a person everything from acne to cancer to memory loss. Although environmental science had never been of interest to Joe, this report sounded serious.

That night as they were getting ready for bed, he shared what he'd learned with Tasha. "While all household appliances put off radiation," he knowingly explained, "electric blankets are the worst. People shouldn't use them. I don't think we should use ours anymore."

"I've never heard that. You can't believe everything you see on TV." She was turning back the sheets.

"It was on *public* television."

"Quit worrying," Tasha said as she climbed into bed. "They couldn't sell them if they were dangerous. Cold as this house is, we'd freeze without that blanket."

"Radiation is bad for a woman's ovaries. Makes 'em shrink up or swell or something." Joe had a hunch ovaries were important.

"Get the light?" She was ignoring him now.

Joe flicked off the light and crawled in next to his wife.

"Mmmm. Doesn't this nice, warm bed feel great?" She snuggled against his back. "Don't worry about all that stuff. Just be glad we have a good blanket to keep us warm. Think how cold we'd be right now without it. Relax. Get some sleep."

Joe tried to put the disturbing report out of his mind. He stretched out but had trouble getting comfortable. He tossed and turned, scrunched and scooted. Something was wrong—his left hand felt funny. Kind of tingly. He took some deep breaths to calm himself, but his whole arm began to feel weird.

Then his ears began to ring, first one, then the other. His tongue started to burn. When he felt as if he could barely breath, Joe kicked off the covers, sprang from the bed, turned on the light, and began frantically searching for the electric-blanket cord.

"Joe! What are you doing?" Tasha said fearfully, her eyes blinking as they adjusted to the light. "Did you hear something?"

He was not going to allow himself to be poisoned by radiation in his own bed, that was what. He groped for the cord.

That's what this was about? Well she was not going to let herself freeze to death in her own bed. He was not going to unplug the blanket.

Finally Joe found the cord. Tasha was right beside him when he did.

The electric blanket was not plugged in.

"Oh," she spoke softly. "I vacuumed last Friday."

"And it's been unplugged . . . ?"

"Ever since."

Joe held up the blanket cord. It had somehow lost its menace.

"You hungry?"

"Sort of."

"Me too. Tuna fish?"

*Enjoy life with your wife.*

ECCLESIASTES 9:9

# FOUR

# All Sold Out

Luke loved going to daycare. Unlike other kids who cried when their mothers left them, Luke could not wait to begin playing. An off-the-charts extrovert, he craved the stimulation of his peers the way other kids long for candy or gum. Playing by himself, or almost as bad—being left with no one but his gentle, quiet-natured mother for company—was for Luke nothing less than torture.

It was not great fun for his mother, Elizabeth, either.

Once they arrived home, although she'd be stressed and tired from her busy day at work, Elizabeth would do her best to entertain Luke with toys and songs and stories. Although comfortable with silence, she worked hard at keeping up a steady stream of talk. Her efforts helped some, but still, many evenings Luke, bored and irritable, carried on over every little thing.

Elizabeth wondered what it was she was doing so wrong. She had other worries too. A single parent for two years, she struggled to make ends meet. While her full-time job provided good benefits, it didn't pay very much, and she and Luke always seemed to run out of money before they did month. Finding ways to fund anything extra had gotten more and more difficult.

So when a friend told her about the perfect part-time job, one that definitely sounded like an answer to prayer, Elizabeth immediately applied and was hired. The Saturday-only position at a doughnut shop just three blocks from her house would give her and Luke a boost of extra cash and not take up a whole weekend. Best of all, she could take Luke to work with her, since day care wasn't open on Saturday.

On the day Elizabeth was hired, Mr. Woo, the shop's owner, went over her duties in great detail. She would need to be there early—no later than 6:00 A.M. She would not be making the doughnuts since they would be ready when she arrived, but she was to run the cash register, keep coffee brewing, and make sure that juice and milk were kept stocked in the front cooler. Most folks took their treats home to eat, but for those who did choose to eat in the tiny shop, Elizabeth was to keep the tables tidy and stocked with napkins. She was also expected to keep the floor swept and the counter free of crumbs.

"Do you understand what to do?" Mr. Woo asked after he had explained her duties.

"Of course, Mr. Woo. No problem. Anything else?"

"When all the doughnuts are gone, hang the 'Sold Out' sign in the window. Then you may lock up and go home."

"You mean the shop doesn't have a regular closing time?" she asked.

"No. You stay until all the doughnuts are gone, or you leave at 5:00, whichever comes first."

"And what time does the shop usually sell out?"

"Sometimes ten, sometimes two. Maybe three or four. Hard to say."

Fair enough. She would see how it went.

Elizabeth had a hunch that Luke would balk at going to the shop, so she began talking it up to him on Friday night. "We're going to do something special tomorrow."

His head popped up. "We are?" *Maybe there would be kids!*

"Yes. First we're going to get up early—so early that it will still be dark outside. Then we're going to take a walk to the doughnut shop. Remember going there?"

"Doughnuts! Goodie!"

"Mommy has a new job at the doughnut shop, and you get to go to work with me. Won't that be fun? We'll pack you a little bag with toys and a blanket and your naptime mat. How does that sound?"

He thought about it for a moment. "Do I get to have chocolate doughnuts?"

"Absolutely."

"With sprinkles?"

"Of course."

"Okay."

And for the first several hours of every Saturday, it *was* okay. Elizabeth liked her new job. The work wasn't hard and business was brisk. The two of them enjoyed getting to know the shop's regular customers. Although many hurried in and out, others lingered at the counter for a leisurely chat. Luke enjoyed these folks; the ones who sat down to eat were the ones who became his real pals. Mostly coffee-drinking codgers, they teased him and gave him quarters and gum.

"Well, hi there. How's my friend Luke this morning?"

"Give me five, buddy."

"New shoes? Wow! I bet you can outrun your mother now."

But when noon approached and the flow of customers slowed, Luke became cranky and bored.

"I wanna go now."

"I know you do, baby. We'll lock up just as soon as we sell all the doughnuts."

"How much longer?"

"Be my helper. Count and see how many of each kind we have left. Can you do that?"

As Mr. Woo had said, closing time was unpredictable. Some Saturdays the two of them arrived home by 11:00. Other days, it was as late as 2:00 or 3:00 before they could lock up and leave. Elizabeth felt ambivalent about late closings. If she sold out early, her check would be smaller. If they stayed until midafternoon, Luke was miserable.

A few months after Elizabeth started working at the shop, she noticed a slowing of sales. She fretted about it, hoping she wasn't doing something wrong. "Warm weather," Mr. Woo explained. "People don't eat as many doughnuts in the spring and summer as in the fall and winter." He cut down on the number of doughnuts he made and instructed Elizabeth to start marking all unsold doughnuts down to half price at noon.

This worked well. Late-arriving customers bought more, and when word got around, folks who hosted afternoon scout meetings or church youth events would stop back after lunch and buy all the remaining doughnuts for half price.

Luke, who delighted in seeing the cases cleaned out, began to watch for such customers. It hadn't taken him long to figure out that these folks were his ticket to freedom. As soon as the clock passed 12:00, he became Mr. Salesman.

He said to a hurried customer. "They're all half price. Wanna buy the rest? Me and my mom get to go home when the doughnuts are all gone. Wanna buy some more?"

To the elderly woman who lived with only a cat, he said, "Seven chocolate and six plain left. Want them all?"

"Luke, that's enough," Elizabeth reprimanded firmly.

Lowering his voice, he spoke convincingly to yet another unsuspecting buyer. "Don't *you* want the rest of the doughnuts?"

One late summer Saturday, a customer unknown to Luke wandered into the shop right at 2:00. Elizabeth was in the back room getting more orange juice, so Luke engaged the man in conversation. Luke told his new friend about how every Saturday he came with his mom to the shop while it was still dark outside, and how they had to stay until all the doughnuts were gone. Today, Luke confided, he and his mom were going to the park when they left the shop. If, that is, they ever got to leave. He rolled his eyes and flung his arm in the direction of the display case. Sales had been slow, and even this late there were lots of doughnuts left.

"Luke!" Elizabeth's chiding voice let him know she'd caught him at it again. She smiled apologetically. "May I help you?"

"Yes." Luke's new friend gazed thoughtfully at the case then glanced over toward Luke. "I'll take everything you have left. Half price, right?"

"Yes," Elizabeth smiled. "Half price."

"Great."

She put the doughnuts in boxes. "Big family?"

"Nope," he grinned, "just me." He stuck out his hand. "Joseph Taylor. I'm the new high-school science teacher."

"Nice to meet you. That'll be seventeen-fifty. Welcome to town. I hope you'll be happy here."

"Thanks."

"Come again."

"I will." He winked at Luke. "Have fun at the park."

Luke and Elizabeth didn't know it then, but that was the last afternoon they would spend in the doughnut shop. On the next Saturday, and the next one, and the one after that, Joseph arrived at exactly noon to buy all of the doughnuts that were left.

*Must have a fast metabolism,* Elizabeth mused. *All those sweets. No one home but him and not a bit overweight.*

Unlike his mother, Luke gave absolutely no thought to his friend's odd eating habits. Each inventory buyout only caused Joseph's worth to grow in Luke's eyes. He began to watch the clock. When it said 12:00 he would go stand at the door of the shop and watch for Joseph. "He's here!" he would announce to his mother when Joseph arrived. Luke counted on his friend to set him free.

And Joseph did not disappoint. Week after week, he bought all of the doughnuts—sometimes a dozen, often as many as six dozen—that were left.

After a few months of acquaintance, it seemed only polite to Elizabeth that she ask Joseph to join her and Luke when they went to the park. After all, the man was new in town. The three of them had such a great time that the next week she invited him to go to the zoo. And the next week? To the county fair.

To reciprocate their kindness, Joseph invited Elizabeth and Luke to his house for dinner and a video. He was a good cook; he made salad and steak. Over a dessert of ice cream, Luke asked his friend to come with them to church. Joseph said that he'd love to go.

Things went on from there. What started out as a cut-rate business transaction blossomed quickly into a full-fledged romance. Months passed, and none of the old codgers, the ones who drank coffee in the shop and kept up with such things, were surprised when Luke told them that he was about to get a new daddy.

Elizabeth was the one who was in for a surprise. Planning the details of their special day, she thought that since they'd met each other at the shop, it would be fitting to serve doughnuts at the wedding reception. Instead of a traditional wedding cake, they could feed each other bites of doughnut. Did Joseph like that idea?

"Not really."

"Why not? It would be cute and romantic, meaningful even."

"Ummm . . . I don't really like doughnuts that much."

Surely she'd misunderstood. "Come on, now. What's this about not liking doughnuts? After all this time—after all the dozens that you've bought? If you don't like doughnuts, why did you come into the shop the first time?"

"Coffee," he said simply. "I was hoping you sold coffee."

Now she understood.

It was a beautiful October wedding. I attended, along with other friends and family and customers from the shop. Elizabeth wore yellow and bronze flowers in her hair, and she and Joseph and Luke held hands while they said their vows. The three of them looked so happy up there, bonded together like the family they were becoming.

*Luke,* I thought to myself as I watched Elizabeth and Joseph kiss, *everything is going to be all right. Best of all, I don't believe you need to worry about selling the leftovers anymore. Your new daddy—well he just went and bought the whole store.*

> *I will declare that your love stands firm forever,*
> *that you established your faithfulness in heaven itself.*
>
> PSALM 89:2

# FIVE

# *The Bread Man*

High fiber.

Low fat.

Vegetarian.

All natural.

Soy.

I'm a sucker for the latest food fad. If it promises to make me and my family healthy, I'm first in line to get signed up. When Oprah hosts Dr. Eat-Strange-Food-And-Live-For-ever, I don't scoff. I buy the man's book. After all, you can't put stuff in a book if it's not true.

My high-nutrient quest started before I saw my children's faces. I traded my beloved coffee for cold milk, my Fruit Loops for old-fashioned oatmeal, and my nitrate-laden bologna for all-natural peanut butter. Once they were born, although I worked part-time and the logistics required for successful breast-feeding proved difficult, I insisted that my little ones subsist on nothing but my own milk.

When my babies grew chubby and ravenous, I learned to make my own baby food. I'd heard that the store-bought foods contained all sorts of icky stuff like starch and sugar, tapioca even. Imagine! The very thought made shivers run up my spine. With self-righteous satisfaction, I spent hours grinding turkey, spinach, yams, and more, into pulverized pulp for my little darlings.

My husband, Randy, on the other hand is a laid-back, easygoing guy. Not much bothers Randy. He worries little and is basically content in whatever state he finds himself. Rarely does the man feel a great compulsion to orchestrate change of any kind.

You've heard it said that opposites attract?

After twenty-plus years of wedded bliss, the two of us have worked out a nearly flawless system. I rant and rave and get all excited and worked up about virtually everything—including my latest health-food crusade. He responds by agreeing with me, making supportive noises, and eating with gusto whatever concoctions I prepare. Although Randy rarely feels the need to voice a strong opinion about anything, when prompted, he's quick to agree that oh yes! he does *indeed* have more energy now that he's eating correctly. Lots more energy. All thanks to me, his wonderful, health-conscious wife.

I do what I can.

I'm really not exaggerating when I say that Randy responds to my healthy-food forays with little complaint. Over the years, in response to various gastronomic gospels, he's eaten seven kinds of beans, tofu, sprouts, even fake chili. He's been switched from chocolate to carob, beef to textured vegetable protein, whole eggs to egg whites—and back again. A man of wise diplomacy, he's learned to nod with grave and appropriate understanding (and maybe relief?) when, in response to yet a different book or article, I declare what was too toxic to eat last week is miraculously the key to good health today.

Randy took issue with only one aspect of my health-food philosophy. When we got married, it came as a great shock to me to discover that this near-perfect man liked—better than any other food in the world—plain, white, square-loafed sandwich bread.

This could not be. Not *my* beloved. Obviously, if I loved the man, if I cared anything about his health, I had to convince him that white bread was not what he needed to be eating. There were the issues of fiber, preservatives, and additives to consider. Serious matters. While he worked at dislodging the top half of his sandwich from the roof of his mouth, I gently explained why I couldn't in good conscience buy white bread for him.

"Whole grains are healthier," I explained. "They lower cholesterol and reduce the risk of some kinds of cancer."

"Cancer doesn't run in my family," he retorted.

"They help clean out the digestive tract."

"My tract is untidy?"

"People in the Bible ate whole grains."

I saw defeat in his eyes.

"Not to worry," I hurriedly explained. "There are all kinds of delicious whole grains to choose from. You'll learn to like them. I promise you will."

I amazed even myself. Not only did I bake and buy whole-grain breads and rolls, I found multigrain crackers and cookies, even biscuits, pancake mix, and tortillas. Our cupboards became a veritable plethora of whole-grain goodness.

And yes, Randy agreed, once you got used to it, chewy whole wheat bread was almost as good as Mrs. Baird's white.

Several years and two kids into our marriage, I was offered the chance to serve on a weeklong medical mission trip to Mexico. Randy couldn't go because of work, and someone needed to stay home with the children. I wondered if it was foolish for me to even consider making such a trip. After all, the children weren't even in school yet. Should I wait until they were older, perhaps until a time when Randy could go with me?

Of course not, my husband assured. I should go. This year. I should answer my call. The three of them would miss me, but they would be fine.

So after stocking the freezer with casseroles, washing all their clothes, arranging baby-sitters, backup baby-sitters, and backups for the backups, I left on the trip. It was wonderful. I loved serving people in such a direct way. I made friends with Christians who, although they didn't speak my language, had much in common with me.

But oh, how I missed my family—especially during the quiet of the night. In the rural area where we worked, telephones were not available, and so for the entire week, I heard nothing from them. I hoped all was well, prayed they were faring all right without me.

I needn't have worried.

Once I was back in Texas, yet still hours from home, I called and talked to Randy and both of the children. They were fine, Randy assured. No one had gotten sick or hurt. Yes, the week had been hectic, and the house was a mess, but nothing tragic had taken place. Hurry on home, he urged. The three of them would be waiting. They'd missed me. They all looked forward to giving me hugs.

What a relief it was to finally see them again. They gave me big bear squeezes and didn't want to let me go. Both children looked like they had grown a foot while I was gone. They needed haircuts, their fingernails trimmed, and their hair washed. My plants needed watering and shelves needed dusting. But as far as I could tell, all had gone according to plan while I was away. The baby-sitters had been there on schedule, people from church had helped out with meals, and my sweet sister-in-law Martha had even done laundry one day.

Only one thing had gone terribly amiss.

The next day after Randy left for work, I stepped into the garage to get some plant food. While there, I poked around, straightened a shelf, and reached to snap the two ill-fitting lids back on to the garbage cans. It was then that the plastic grocery-store bag caught my eye. It was in the very bottom of an otherwise empty garbage can, so I'd almost not seen it. Unusually curious—rarely do I feel compelled to go through my family's trash—I set the plant food down, picked up the bag, untied it, and peeked inside.

No.

It couldn't be.

Surely not.

Not *my* husband!

I dropped the bag like it was a bomb and tore into the house to call my friend June. I simply had to share my disappointment with someone.

"Annette," she spoke gently. "These things happen. Randy's not the first man to take advantage of his wife's being out of town."

"But the children—they were right there in the house."

"I know. I know." June offered comfort, then dared to ask, "Annette, what exactly was it that you found? Empty liquor bottles?"

"No."

"Cigarettes?"

"No."

"Cigar stubs?"

"No."

"One of *those* magazines?"

"Oh, no. Not that."

"Then what?" she asked gently. "You can tell me."

"Bread wrappers," I blurted out. "Mrs. Baird's. White. Five of them."

I never told Randy that I was on to his clandestinely consumed carbs. To this day, he thinks he got away with eating five loaves of white bread that week and that I am none the wiser.

But Randy is wrong. I am wiser. After making my discovery and giving it some thought, I drove to the store and loaded my cart with both wheat and white bread. When I served him white bread at dinner that night, he looked at me with a question in his eyes.

"New research," I explained. "White bread turns out to be not so bad after all."

"Really?" he exclaimed, trying hard not to look too pleased.

"Really."

*She brings him good, not harm,*
*all the days of her life.*

PROVERBS 31:12

# SIX

# Ice Cream for Breakfast

My friend Melissa looks like a model. So does her husband, Mark. Actually, the two of them favor each other a bit—in that drop-dead gorgeous sort of way. Friends and family are not surprised that the genetic mix of Melissa and Mark produced a batch of really cute kids. Should you run into them, whether it be at church on a Sunday morning or at a picnic on a Saturday afternoon, you can be sure that Melissa and Mark, along with seven-year-old Isabelle and three-year-old twins Geoffrey and Isaac, will look like they've just stepped off the pages of a fashion magazine.

All five members of the family have golden blond hair—the children's with curls—and doe-like chestnut-brown eyes framed by nicely shaped brows and thick, curly lashes. The entire bunch is also blessed with straight white teeth and healthy skin that, instead of burning and peeling like the rest of ours, mellows into a smooth and even tan at the first hint of summer sun.

Melissa makes looking good appear easy. She knows how to mix and match outfits and how to put colors together. She loves clothes and loves to dress her family well. Every December when I get Melissa's Christmas-photo card, I marvel at how put-together her family looks. Unlike my clan's funny-looking holiday photos, no one in Melissa's picture has even one hair out of place. No one is drooling, no one's shirttail is hanging out, and nobody appears to be missing important buttons.

What is most amazing about Melissa is that she has learned to clothe all of them beautifully on a shoestring budget. It wasn't easy for her at first.

Growing up in a wealthy Southern family, she had practically everything she wanted.

Clothes? Melissa had her own charge card at Neiman Marcus before she started tenth grade.

Cars? Her daddy gave her a new white Camaro when she turned sixteen.

Vacations? The family went skiing in the winter, to the beach in the summer, and traveled to Europe every other spring.

When Melissa and Mark announced their engagement, many folks predicted that it would be difficult for Melissa to adjust to a moderate lifestyle. Mark, a teacher, would never make much money, and Melissa was hardly accustomed to doing without. Money problems have broken up many a marriage, the couple was warned. Be sure you know exactly what it is that you're getting yourself into.

Right. Like any of us do.

All in all, Melissa has adjusted quite well, I think. It doesn't bother her to drive a beat-up van, and she knows at least twenty-three tricks to fixing delicious dinners with ground beef. She buys her makeup at Wal-Mart and her cleaning products at Sam's. Vacations are spent camping out, and pizza from the buffet is a much-anticipated family treat.

But there is one luxury that Melissa has refused to give up, and that is the yearly family portrait. All during childhood Melissa enjoyed the ritual of a once-a-year formal family portrait session. She and her parents and her brother and sisters would get all dressed up for the family photographer's visit to their home. Her mother saw to it that each of her children was dressed in a coordinating outfit, that the setting was as lovely as it could be, and that they all smiled their best. Year after year, the results were stunning.

It gives Melissa great pleasure to point out to her own children the photographs that show her at their same ages. She enjoys looking at the changing hairstyles her mother wore and studying the way the photos chronicle her and her siblings' infancies, childhoods, and teen years. They are Melissa's favorite family treasure, and so it is only natural that she desires to leave her children the same kind of memories.

And so all year long, by carving any corner not already cut, Melissa saves for the family's special Christmas photo session. Kmart's studios won't do; neither will she settle for JCPenney's personal portrait plan. Not even Olan Mills is deemed good enough. No, the family must troop into a real studio, to a real (expensive) photographer. That once-a-year family portrait is Melissa's pride and joy, so she is willing to sacrifice all year long in order to enjoy the services of a professional.

Melissa's mother contributes to the cause. Not with money for the portrait, mind you—Mark and Melissa decided long ago that they would make do financially without assistance from her parents—but with clothes for the children. Ever since Isabelle was born, Melissa's mother has purchased designer outfits for each of the children as part of her Christmas gift to the family.

Every November Melissa anticipates the arrival of that package. When it finally shows up at the post office, she is barely able to wait until she gets home to open it. Whatever

outfits her mother has picked, one thing is for sure: They will be absolutely exquisite.

This year is no exception.

Melissa opens the box and lifts out forest-green velvet and red-plaid taffeta brother-sister outfits for all three of her children. She studies Isabelle's dress first. It has a fitted bodice, covered buttons, and a white Battenberg lace collar set off by a wide, plaid taffeta sash. The boys' coordinating outfits are matching velvet knickers, crisp, white cotton shirts, velvet bow ties, and plaid taffeta vests. Melissa's mother, as she thoughtfully does every year, includes tights for Isabelle, socks for Geoffrey and Isaac, and new black shoes for all three.

"Oh, Mother," Melissa gushes over the phone to her mother. "The outfits are too precious. I love them! They're even more beautiful than last year. Thank you so much!"

When Mark gets home from work, she shows him the children's new clothes, and he does his best to act suitably impressed. Yes, he agrees, Isabelle, Geoffrey, and Isaac will look wonderful when they go to have their picture taken. Only one thing he questions. "*Knickers?* Aren't the boys getting a bit old for such sissy little pants?"

Melissa gives him a playful swat. "Don't you dare let them hear you say that!" she threatens. "With their golden curls, my three babies will look like something out of a storybook. This will be our nicest family portrait yet. You'll see."

"You just tell me where and when to show up," Mark answers with a grin.

"It's all set up. One week from Saturday at 3:00. Don't worry, I'll remind you."

"I was afraid of that. My favorite event of the season. Be still my heart."

She throws a pillow at his head.

It is Friday night, past 10:00. Melissa has just returned home after unexpectedly leaving town on Wednesday. Melissa's best friend, who lives in the next town, needed emergency surgery. With a husband working overseas, no relatives in town, and two small children, her friend was in such a bind that Melissa went to help her out. She stayed until her friend's family arrived.

"I'm so glad to be home," she greets Mark at the door. "Miss me? Kids okay?" She stretches and yawns.

"Everybody's fine. Course we missed you. About time you came home." Mark pulls her into his arms and gives her a nice homecoming kiss.

"Think I'll look in on the kids. How long have they been asleep?"

"At least an hour. Maybe more."

Melissa tiptoes into Isabelle's room first. She smiles when she spies her daughter's new Christmas dress hanging from the closet door. As she bends to touch the little girl's cheek, she whispers, "Get lots of beauty sleep, little one. Picture day's tomorrow."

Then Melissa steps into the twins' room. Although they each have a bed, the boys usually choose to sleep together. Careful not to wake them, Melissa steps over a toy, picks a sock up off the floor, then pulls back the covers for a peek at their chubby cheeks.

No! It can't be. Both of them?

She yelps for Mark to come here right now.

"Honey," she's trying to whisper, "what is this? My babies! What happened to their hair?"

"I cut it."

"You cut their hair?" Melissa's trying not to cry. "Mark, they're practically bald. I can see skin! What were you thinking?"

"I don't know." He shrugs. "They were with me in the bathroom while I was using the clippers to clean up my neck. They asked me to cut their hair like their friend Jimmy's. Remember? Jimmy has a buzz."

"And it is ugly!" Melissa interrupts him. Luckily the children are sound sleepers because she's fuming by now. "Let me get this straight. You shaved my babies' heads because they *wanted* you to? Tomorrow is picture day! *Picture day.* And two of my three beautiful babies look like skinheads. Mark, since when do we as parents do anything for our children because they *want* us to?"

He doesn't know.

"If the boys wanted to jump off a bridge, you'd let them? If they asked you to let them drive the car, you'd hand them the keys? If they told you they wanted to eat ice cream for breakfast, you'd give them a spoon? Mark, what were you thinking?"

He guesses not much.

Well, she just guesses that he can sleep on the couch.

The next morning Melissa rolls over like she does every morning to snuggle up to Mark's warm back. But he isn't there. The memory of last night's outburst flies over her in a rush. What got into her? Poor Mark. Melissa can't believe she made such a big deal over something as silly as haircuts. She has some apologizing to do.

"Honey?" she calls from beneath the cozy covers.

Unexpectedly, two little heads pop up over the side of the bed.

"Hi, Mommy," her bald boys say with grins on their faces.

"Hi, boys."

"Daddy gave us haircuts."

"I see that."

They grin at her some more.

"Mommy?"

"Yes, darling?"

"We want ice cream for breakfast."

Mark chuckles from the door.

Melissa looks first into the twinkling eyes of her handsome husband, then into the bright faces of her two young sons. She pauses only a second before pulling them up into the bed with a two-armed swoop. "Sure you do." She tickles their tummies, rubs their ragged heads. "And Isabelle, too. Run wake her up. This is Saturday; let's have breakfast in bed. Chocolate, peach, or cookies and cream?"

When I received Melissa's Christmas-photo card this year, I took notice of the lovely setting, the softly reflected light, the beautiful red-and-green outfits her children wore. As always, it's a beautiful picture. An especially cute touch, I think, are the little black baseball caps perched on the boys' heads.

*The end of a matter is better than its beginning,*
*and patience is better than pride.*

ECCLESIASTES 7:8

# SEVEN

# Fishin' for a Feller

Eighty-one-year-old Annie Kate McGarity misses all her late husbands. However, it is Floyd, her first, that she misses most of all on those warm spring days when she knows, from years of cane-pole experience, that the fish will be biting. Granted, she misses him on holidays like Thanksgiving and Christmas, anniversaries, and birthdays, but the pain of those occasions don't compare with the pain that Annie Kate feels at the loss of her fishing partner.

When Annie Kate first married Floyd, she didn't know one thing about lines or floats or how to bait a hook. Truth be told, she had no real desire to learn. Annie Kate's mama taught her that a proper woman's place was in the house; well, maybe on the porch late of an afternoon, but definitely always well out of the sun. A woman's place was certainly not on the muddy bank of some lake or river. A lady, Annie

Kate could hear her mother's voice saying, would never even go near a minnow or a worm.

But then Annie Kate's mother wasn't married to an outdoorsman like Floyd.

On Annie Kate and Floyd's second morning as husband and wife, Floyd woke her up, bringing her coffee in bed. "Honey? Rise and shine. Let's have some breakfast and go see if they're biting."

Biting? She rubbed her eyes.

"Sugar, I've got a real nice surprise for you. Wake up and see."

Eighteen-year-old Annie Kate loved surprises. She sat up in bed, drew her knees to her chin.

"What is it, Floyd?"

Stepping aside, he revealed exactly what it was—her very own fishing pole.

"That's not all." Floyd was as excited as a child. "Look right here. I got you this little folding camp stool and some rubber boots, too. Sure hope they fit." He grinned ear to ear.

At first Annie Kate could not get the hang of it. Over and over again she'd fling her line out over the water just like Floyd showed her. But unlike him, she'd get her hook hung up on something or other. She'd tug and yank, which only made things worse. Each time Floyd, fishing up the bank a ways, would look down and see what a mess she'd gotten herself into, he'd lay his own pole down and unsnag her line. Not even once that honeymoon week did he act impatient with her.

"Try to toss it out easy, like this," he suggested sweetly.

It took more than that week, but in time, Annie Kate learned to love fishing. Sitting on a bank beside Floyd every weekend, she got pretty good at it too. Within a year of her marriage to Floyd, Annie Kate was proficient with a rod and reel.

Catching fish was a newly acquired skill, but Annie Kate had always loved to eat them. Floyd, too. Except for what they gave away, the two of them consumed all they caught—neither one minded having fish several times a week. Annie Kate and Floyd had even worked out a system: She cleaned the fish (the blood and mess made Floyd gag), and he (being the better cook) fried them up in a skillet of grease.

Having no children made it easy for Annie Kate and Floyd to pack up and go somewhere almost every weekend. To avoid the expense of staying in motels, they slept on the ground in an army-issue canvas tent. It worked fine while they were young, but as they got older, their backs got fussy about the nights spent on the ground. So when Floyd retired he went out and bought a pop-up camper to take on trips. Not much bigger than a kitchen table, the camper had only enough room for the two of them to stretch out. No matter, because sleeping on a real mattress felt so good they thought they'd died and gone to heaven.

During the fifty-one years that Annie Kate and Floyd were married, they took advantage of holidays, long weekends, and vacations and dropped their hooks in nearly every body of water in Texas and lots of places in Arkansas and Oklahoma, too.

Fish and game laws vary from state to state, and penalties can be stiff for those who don't abide by the rules. It was in an Oklahoma state park that Annie Kate became part of the criminal element. Since the fish had not been biting enough to make it worth their trouble, the two of them had left the lake and had gone back to their campsite early. Like he always did, Floyd opened the bucket and took a peek at what they'd caught. "This one yours?" he said as he pointed to a certain fish.

Annie Kate believed it was.

"Looks small."

Annie Kate studied the fish. "You're right. Too small. I should've thrown him back."

"Hope the game warden doesn't pay us a visit."

"Me neither. Hot day like this, the man's probably resting in the shade somewhere. I sure could use a cold drink. How about you?"

They both pulled the tabs on RC Colas.

It wasn't ten minutes later that Floyd and Annie Kate looked up to see the game warden a ways down the trail, but definitely headed their way.

"Shoot," said Floyd. "Look who's coming to pay a visit. Maybe he won't check the bucket. Doggone it . . . Annie Kate, what do you think you're doing?"

At first sight of the uniformed officer, Annie Kate sprang from her seat. Turning her back to the trail, she grabbed the small fish and stuffed it down the front of her swimsuit. As the warden approached their camp, she smiled at him demurely and topped her suit with one of Floyd's big button-down shirts.

"Afternoon, folks," the game warden said. "Just making my rounds." Honoring Annie Kate's hasty attempt at modesty, he took care to look at Floyd as he spoke.

"Afternoon, sir," Floyd answered. "Floyd Rollins. My wife, Annie Kate. Mighty hot today. Have a seat, won't you? Rest here in the shade for a spell."

"Nice to meet you folks. I'm Officer Plunket. And thanks, don't mind if I do."

"Cold drink?" invited Annie Kate.

"Yes, ma'am. That'd be real nice." The warden took a seat and mopped his brow. "Where y'all from? Noticed the Texas plates on your truck."

When Annie Kate handed him the drink, Officer Plunket saw the twitch. He observed it a second time when she took a seat near her husband, and yet a third time when she tried to tell him where it was they were from.

Bless her sweet heart, thought the warden. Her husband's, too. Sad condition for a woman to be in. A tic of some kind, he guessed—looked to be the same kind of problem his great-aunt Flo had. He tried not to stare. Why, his poor aunt Flo, she couldn't do much of anything but sit in the house with her feet up. These things only got worse, he knew.

"Nice to meet you folks." He rose to go. "Enjoy the rest of your stay in the park. Drive careful on your way home."

"Thank you, sir. We will."

"Just one more thing, Mr. Rollins."

"Yes, sir?"

"I need to take a look at all you've caught today."

"Of course." Floyd showed him to the bucket.

The game warden peered in the bucket, and with a tip of his hat, he was gone.

As soon as the man was out of sight, Floyd turned to Annie Kate. "Pee-ew, honey, you don't smell too good!"

Although Trina has been volunteering at the nursing home for several months, she has not had the courage to take any of the residents out. She thought that now was a good time to start.

"Mrs. McGarity, would you like to come spend the day with me on Thursday?"

"Why, I'd love to! Now, what did you say your name was, dear?"

At Trina's house, Annie Kate wanted to see every room.

"What a pretty bedspread. And pillows to match!"

"You've got a nice big kitchen, honey. Plenty of cabinet space."

"This your little girl's room? Now, isn't it nice."

After Annie Kate explored the house, they had tea and cookies and talked about the weather and their families.

"What does your husband do?" asked Mrs. McGarity.

"He owns a hardware store."

"You know, I've had three husbands. Outlived them all. I miss having a husband. I wouldn't mind taking on another one," she sipped her tea and winked, "if you know what I mean."

"Excuse me?"

"Do you like to fish? Well, I do. I miss fishing so much. Floyd and me used to fish all the time. My other two husbands fished too. Honey, I'm telling you, if I could find me another good man, I'd marry him—but only if he could fish."

Trina thought maybe she should change the subject. "Would you like to look at some pictures?" She got out three heavy albums. "This is my husband, Matthew. Here's our little girl, Sandy, on her third birthday." She turned the page. "That one? Oh, that's Matthew's family. It was taken at his cousin's wedding last spring. Look at the bride. Isn't she pretty?"

Mrs. McGarity studied the photo and asked about each person in turn.

"Who's this man?"

"That's Matthew's dad."

"Where's his wife?"

"Well, you see, it's real sad. She passed away last year—"

Mrs. McGarity interrupted, "Nice looking man. Kind of on the short side though, wouldn't you say?"

"Well, no, ma'am. He's at least five foot—"

"Does he have his own teeth?"

"I'm not sure, but he is in good health. He lives with Matthew's sister in a town near . . ."

Mrs. McGarity looked at the picture a bit closer and murmured to herself, "Not too bad." A bit louder, "Honey, does he like to fish?"

Over the years I've read oodles of books, gone to count-less seminars, and bought dozens of tapes, all in the quest to improve my marriage. Don't get me wrong, it's not that Randy and I don't enjoy perfect wedded bliss every day of our lives; I just think it's important for a person to keep up.

I doubt that Annie Kate McGarity has read any of those books. She's had no training in counseling or psychology that I know of. Yet when it comes to seeking a mate, I think she may be on to something: Marry a man who likes to fish.

Think about it.

Fishermen know better than to muddy the waters. You'll never catch them throwing rocks and rarely do they try to make waves.

Fishermen do not expect to be entertained all the time. They realize that sitting and shootin' the breeze is something two people can enjoy doing together.

Fishermen are not surprised when things get tangled up. While they are usually very good at getting things unsnagged, they're not opposed to cutting a line and starting over fresh.

Need yet another reason to seek out someone who likes to fish?

Here's the real secret: A fisherman is someone who's not afraid to get hooked!

*The LORD God said, "It is not good for the man to be alone. I will make a helper suitable for him."*

GENESIS 2:18

EIGHT

# Grand Exit

It was on a weekday afternoon, over the sound of a Hoover vacuum cleaner, that my twenty-year-old husband-to-be, Randy, broke the news to his mother.

"Mom," he said to her back, "just thought I'd let you know that Annette and I have decided to move to Colorado right after the wedding."

"What did you say?" She was busy trying to clean in a corner and didn't even look up.

"We're moving to Colorado—Annette and I," Randy repeated over the roar.

This time she heard. Stunned, she stopped and unplugged the cord, then just stood there for a moment, open-mouthed.

"When did you decide this?" she finally asked.

"Today," Randy told her. "Annette's always wanted to live in the mountains. See you later, Mom. We've got class."

"Bye, Mrs. Smith," I said sweetly as we left.

Randy was my mother-in-law's oldest child, the first of her three to leave the Texas nest. I wonder now, What were we thinking?

"You'd think someone died, the way she's carrying on."

"Some mothers have no life outside of their children."

"After all, a mother's job *is* to prepare her children to leave."

When we were younger, more tired moms, my friends and I could not understand all the fuss about empty nests. Honestly, the thought of having grown-up, independent children—kids able to wipe their own noses and buckle themselves into seatbelts—sounded absolutely delicious. Up to our gizzards in carpools and cupcakes, diaper rashes and booster shots, we could not wait to have a little time to ourselves. We dreamed of the day when we would read the morning newspaper without stopping to clean up spilled milk. We longed for the day when we could take a bath without an audience. And, oh, for the day when we could cook with onions and mushrooms and other stuff deemed yucky by our kids.

The old ladies in our neighborhoods and the older moms at our churches begged us to treasure those fleeting child-rearing years. They warned us that the scant time we had with our children would be over before we knew it. They cautioned us about pushing our kids to grow up too fast.

Did we listen?

Not really.

When our babies were in our arms, we wanted them to crawl.

When they crawled, we couldn't wait for them to walk.

When they walked, we wanted them to run.

Not until the day we realized that our suddenly grown-up children were about to fling themselves headlong into the world did we reverse our desires and shamelessly beg them to slow down, take their time, and not be in such a great rush to leave home.

A year and a half ago my oldest chick and only son, Russell, flew the coop two days after his high-school graduation. Eager to be out on his own, Russell had applied for and was awarded a job at an across-the-state Christian youth camp. (Lest anyone forget, Texas is a really big state!)

But that was not all. After working all summer, Russell planned to come home for only a few days in early August, then leave again to go to a university eight hours away, in a whole different state.

Russell's senior year of high school was a busy one, and it wasn't until May that it hit me: For all practical purposes my oldest baby was leaving home for good. No longer would I see him, boss him, chat with him every day. I was not prepared for the emotions his graduation provoked in me. The overwhelming grief I felt at the thought of him leaving was a total shock. After all, I'd raised my son to be an independent person. I'd known for years that he'd likely go away to school, and I had supported him in his efforts to stretch his wings. And shouldn't it have counted for something that, aside from being a wife and a mom, I had a busy, fulfilling life of my own?

Maybe it should have; but I'm telling you, it didn't.

Oh, I worked hard at putting on a good face. Not desiring for a minute to dampen Russell's happiness, I pretended to be relaxed and nonchalant about his pending departure. "Follow your dreams," I told him. "You are going to have so much fun! Need any help packing?" I longed to be a hip, modern sort of mom. No matter how raw I felt inside, I did my best to maintain my façade.

I think I did pretty well. For a while anyway.

On the day Russell planned to leave for the camp, his dad got up and left for work extra early. (And they say that men are so brave.) I stayed behind, puttering in the house, and aimed to leave for my own job just a few minutes before Russell pulled his well-packed little car out of our drive. I thought it was a great plan. That way I was not going to be left standing alone in the yard, waving good-bye to my son. I knew better.

So when Russell had everything loaded in his car, when I was sure he was within minutes of pulling out, I gave him a hug and a kiss, slipped him twenty dollars, got into my car, and drove myself to work.

*There now,* I breathed behind the wheel. *That wasn't so bad.* The key, I decided, was to pretend that Russell was just leaving town for one night. He'd done that many times before. I began to believe I would be just fine.

And I was, for a good fifteen minutes.

It was not until I was at work in the crowded front office, making copies at the machine, that I lost it.

"Annette, are you all right?" my twenty-five-year-old boss asked.

I could feel the muscles in my face contort.

"Are you sick or something?"

I could not say a word.

"You look sort of funny. Is everything okay?"

Finally, I shook my head no.

"Annette? What is it?"

"Wahhhhh!"

I was so embarrassed by my tears (I'm usually *so* together, you see) that all I wanted to do was crawl into a hole. Seeing as how there was no good place to hide, and seeing as how a weeping nurse is not much good to anyone, my gentle-spirited, rather shaken young boss told me I should take the day off.

Gladly. I got into my car and headed back home. There, I knew, I would no longer have to hold it all in. With my husband at work, my daughter at school, and Russell, by now, well down the road, I could fling myself across the bed and wail and sob to my heart's content.

There was just one wrinkle in my plan. When I turned onto my street, Russell's car was in the driveway. He had not left yet.

I had nowhere to hide.

One week after Randy and I married, we did indeed move to Colorado. Why? Because we'd heard it was pretty, I guess. That and the fact that I thought it sounded terribly romantic to tell folks that, yes, my new husband and I were moving to the mountains.

It was on a clear Monday morning, after we'd packed all our wedding presents into a tiny U-Haul trailer, that Randy and I said our good-byes to the family. Not unexpectedly, the occasion of our departure prompted a dreary, teary, drawn-out driveway drama.

Yes, we would be careful.

Yes, we would write.

Good-bye.

And yes, of course. We would call the moment we arrived.

As Randy steered our jam-packed car and trailer away from his parents' home and eased it toward the north-headed highway that would deliver us to the Rockies, he and I giggled that we'd made our great escape. After all, as a married couple he and I were grown-ups, out on our own, able to make all our own decisions. How wonderful it was to realize that from now on we would be directing our own paths, answering to no one but each other. Colorado, better get ready, because here we come!

*Pft . . . pft . . . pft . . .*

Suddenly there was this loud popping sound, apparently coming from the car's engine. Next a strong, stinky odor. Then puffs of rising gray smoke. Finally a red light inside the car came on.

All of this and we had yet to reach the edge of town.

"Is something wrong?" I asked my new husband.

He wasn't sure.

"Should we pull over?"

He guessed maybe so.

"What's wrong with the car?"

He didn't know.

*He didn't know?* I thought all husbands knew about cars.

"Annette," he finally assured me, "as I see it we've got two choices here."

Such a capable man I'd married. It was obvious he knew just what to do.

"My dad or yours? Which one of them should we call to tow us in?"

> Generations come and generations go,
> but the earth remains forever.
> The sun rises and the sun sets,
> and hurries back to where it rises.
> The wind blows to the south
> and turns to the north;
> round and round it goes,
> ever returning on its course.
> All streams flow into the sea,
> yet the sea is never full.
> To the place the streams come from,
> there they return again.
>
> ECCLESIASTES 1:4–7

Part 2

*A Friend Loves at All Times*

# NINE

# And to All a Good Night

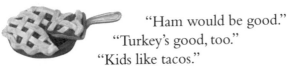

"Ham would be good."

"Turkey's good, too."

"Kids like tacos."

"What about dessert?"

Ruth Ann Brumley, the church's chairperson of this year's Christmas party for children with imprisoned parents, sneaked a peek at her watch. At this rate, they'd be chatting all night. With only three weeks until the event, this bunch of party planners did not have the luxury of wasting any time.

She politely interrupted the group's leisurely discussion. "Say, how about we divide up into four committees: food, decorations, entertainment, and gifts. We don't all have to be involved in every decision."

"Sounds like a good idea."

"Okay by me."

"Good. Julie, can you and Marge and Ellen plan the food? Sandra, Paul, and Allen, how about decorations? Tom and

Sarah, can you decide what to do about gifts? Ellie and Becky—entertainment? Great. Whatever you come up with will be fine by me. Let's meet back next Sunday and see how we're all coming along."

And happily, by the next Sunday everything *was* coming along. The food committee had decided on a turkey dinner with all the trimmings, and the decorating committee was going with red and silver. The gift committee, after much discussion back and forth, had determined that each child would receive one nice toy, a stocking stuffed with candy and trinkets, and one practical item of clothing. The gifts, donated by various Sunday school classes around the city, would be presented in the names of the incarcerated parents. The entertainment committee was actively pursuing a recently retired out-of-town magician.

"Is he willing to come?" asked Ruth Ann.

"Looks like. We'll know for sure by Tuesday."

"Wonderful. Good work, all of you. Thanks for your help. One more detail. We'll need a Santa."

No one volunteered.

"All right then, see you next Sunday." Ruth Ann made a mental note. She'd need to locate and draft someone to play Santa Claus.

Weeks before, when asked by her pastor to coordinate this year's party (a different local church hosted the event every year), Ruth Ann had committed herself without giving much thought to the task. She was a seasoned PTA room mother, a multilevel Girl Scout leader, and a ten-year Vacation Bible School veteran, so throwing a simple children's Christmas party wouldn't even be a challenge. She knew the holiday routine well: Hang some streamers and decorate a tree; blow up a few balloons; set out cookies and punch (clear punch, never red); lead at least two games; and finally, direct the children in the singing of a few familiar Christmas carols. It was always best to wait to announce the surprise visit from Santa until just before it was time to pack up the kids and send them home. By then you could be sure they'd be sugar-loaded and hyper.

With good planning, the whole event wouldn't last longer than an hour and a half. All evidence of the party would be cleaned up, and she'd be home by nine.

Then between Sunday school and the church service, Ruth Ann was handed the list of those who'd be coming to the party. "You've got the children's names, as well as some helpful information about each of them," her pastor explained. "Let me know if you need my assistance."

"Don't worry about a thing," she said with a smile.

Settling into a pew, half-listening to what seemed like an endless recital of church activity announcements, Ruth Ann pulled the list from where she'd tucked it between the pages of her Bible. She unfolded it and scanned the page.

*Christina, age four. Likes dolls and storybooks. Wears a size three.*

*Elliot, age nine. Loves to draw. Likes country music. Wears a size ten.*

*Jason and Marcie, twins, age seven . . .*

Beside each child's name and description was typed the name of the parent who was in prison. Most of these were of men, but some were women, mothers who would not be spending Christmas with their little ones. Most notable of all were eight out of the twenty-seven children who, according to the list, had *both* of their parents in prison.

All alone at Christmas. She'd had no idea.

Ruth Ann refolded the list and tucked it into her purse. She blew her nose, wiped her eyes, and opened her hymnbook and tried to sing. She couldn't. Forget cookies and clear punch, she decided, sitting up straighter. Forget silly games and off-key carols. Forget saving Santa until the end. Forget getting home by nine. This was going to be a *party.*

There would be real food. Loud music. Live entertainment. Santa could stay all night. And the children would have *red* punch. As much as they wanted.

Ruth Ann Brumley was going to need some help!

She got it. Her chosen committee members, each of them moved by the lonely plight of the children and determined that their young guests be treated to a night they'd never forget, were going to go all out. With each meeting, the reports of what they had planned grew more and more elaborate. Even so, on the night of the party Ruth Ann could not believe what the volunteers had done.

Red and silver candles, hanging garlands, gigantic shiny balls, and strings of tiny twinkling lights had transformed the utilitarian church fellowship hall into a glittering palace. Not one, but three towering Christmas trees wafted forth a fragrance that, when mingled with the aroma of roasted turkey and homemade yeast rolls, made a person think that her nose had died, gone on to heaven, and left the rest of her behind.

Turkey (unwilling that *any* child be disappointed, committee members had prepared two dozen extra drumsticks), ham, stuffing, three kinds of potatoes, salads, gravy, vegetables, fruits, and pies were spread on the buffet table draped with a red velvet cloth. An ice sculpture of Rudolph, surrounded by decorated cakes and whipped-cream-topped puddings, was flanked by a rented ice-cream machine primed to dispense both chocolate and vanilla into cups and cones.

The church's adult men's choir and the young people's concert bell choir stood ready in their robes, scheduled to perform at preset times so as to give the main musician—a professional harpist—occasional breaks throughout the evening.

Not only was the tuxedo-clad magician pumped to perform that night, he also was donating his time and had brought along friends. When first contacted and told the nature of the party, he helpfully offered to recruit not only a juggler and a cartoon-portrait artist, but his cousin the fortune teller and an old pal who owned three well-behaved dogs that did tricks. Slightly overwhelmed by so many entertainment options, committee members told the man that while they were truly grateful, they'd pass on the fortune-teller cousin and the dogs, lest the children get too excited.

As she surveyed the hall, Ruth Ann was acutely aware that this night would be the only Christmas celebration many of the children would experience. Had everything turned out all right? She thought so. Would the children have fun? She hoped so. *Please God,* she prayed, *let them have a good time. On this of all nights, let them know they are loved and special.*

Then the children began to arrive, accompanied by grandmothers, aunts and uncles, foster parents, moms, and dads. They were darling children, scrubbed and eager children, wide-eyed, giggling, ready-for-fun children. Ruth Ann, stationed near the hall's entrance, felt her heart swell as she overheard their comments.

"Wow! Look at all those Christmas trees!"

"When do we eat?"

"That guy can juggle!"

"Where's Santa?"

*Santa. Santa? No!* Ruth Ann couldn't believe it. How could she have forgotten? He'd been on her list. She'd meant to call someone, thought about calling someone, but remembered with a wave of nausea that she had never gotten around to calling someone! There *was* no Santa.

Slipping away from the party, Ruth Ann raced down the hall to the church storage room. Digging through outdated choir robes and boxes of puppet-ministry props, she prayed and prayed and tried not to panic. *I know I saw a Santa suit in here. Please let it still be here. Please, please, please.* Relief made her knees go weak when finally, wedged between a stack of folding chairs and a mountain of frayed carpet remnants, she located the suit, the hat, and even the beard.

*Thank you, Jesus!* she prayed. Then from behind her came an unexpected scraping sound. Startled, Ruth Ann stood up, bumped her head on an overhead shelf, and sank back down.

"Ouch!"

"*Señora?* You okay? Can I help you?" Pedro, the church custodian, spoke with a thick accent from the doorway.

"No, not now . . . I mean, yes, I do need help . . . could you possibly . . . ?"

"*Sí?*" The man extended his hand.

After a welcome speech by Ellen (since Ruth Ann was nowhere to be found) and a prayer by Paul, the children were given free run of the hall, instructed only to have lots of fun. They did not have to be told twice.

As the adult volunteers mingled among them, Jason and Marcie ate two drumsticks each, and Jackson, Sidney, and Ben played follow-the-leader between the Christmas trees. Ashley and Rosie lined up for ice cream while Elliot, Tyrone, and Beth sang along with the choir. Samantha and Tara gently stroked the harp as Christina and Marcus had their cartoon portraits drawn. Matt, Justin, and Rebecca cheered when the magician pulled a rabbit from his hat while Emily and Grant tried to learn to juggle.

Finally the most anticipated guest of the evening made a quiet entrance through a side door. It didn't take long for the group of children to spot the red-suited gentleman. Everything else in the room was forgotten, and they crowded around his feet.

"Santa!" they squealed. "It's Santa Claus! He's here! He's really here!"

Once Santa took a seat, the children came one by one to perch on his knee and whisper in his ear. He smiled and nodded and gave them all hugs. If any of them noticed that he was a man of very few words ("ho, ho, ho" made up his vocabulary), they didn't show it. Once they were ready to get down, he gave them each a goodie-stuffed stocking and Ruth Ann snapped their picture with a Polaroid camera. She'd prepared little frames so they could each have a momento to take home with them.

Conspicuous amid all that fun was one dark-eyed little girl who didn't join in. Tempted by none of the activities, not even by Santa, three-year-old Maria remained in her seat. Even her food sat untouched on her plate.

Ellen noticed and tried to help. "Does she speak English?" she asked the girl's foster mom.

The foster mom said yes, so Ellen walked over to the girl and asked, "What's wrong, sweetheart? Aren't you hungry?"

No response.

"Want some pie?"

Nothing.

"Did you see Santa Claus?"

Still no response.

"She's only been with us three days," Maria's foster mother whispered. "Hasn't said a word since she arrived. Misses her mom, I'm sure."

When all the children had taken their turns, Santa rose from his chair, straightened his belt and his beard, and moved slowly toward little Maria. For the past half hour he'd been frequently glancing in her direction. He knelt beside her chair.

She didn't look up.

He placed a stocking in her lap.

She didn't move.

"*Hola,*" he whispered in her native tongue.

Her head popped up as if drawn by a string.

"*Qué pasa?*" he asked.

Her eyes got wide and she slid out of her chair.

"*Cómo te llamas?*"

"Maria," she answered, no longer shy.

"*Me llamo Papá Noel.*"

It seemed like the rest of the party just melted away and it was just the two of them alone in the room. No twinkling lights, no decorated trees, no magicians or musicians. Maria, cuddled comfortably on Santa's lap, finally feeling understood, began to talk. And talk. And talk.

All over the hall, eyes watched the pair. For a few seconds, the noise in the room quieted. Everyone, even the children, seemed to sense that something very special had happened.

It was, after all, the season for such things.

It's now spring, and from what I hear from Ruth Ann, Maria is still talking, giggling, and playing and is even learning to sing. Ruth Ann keeps up with almost all of the children. After the holidays she began volunteering her time with the organization that helps kids like Maria. Easter's in a few weeks and—no surprise—Ruth Ann is planning a big party. And what about Pedro? Since the party, he has become Ruth Ann's number one volunteer. No matter what Ruth Ann's kids need, Pedro is the man for the job.

I think Maria would certainly agree.

*Whoever welcomes one of these little children in my name welcomes me.*

MARK 9:37

TEN

# Dyeing for a Friend

Janet Reece changed her mind about liking school the same year that coloring stopped being a subject. By the beginning of first grade, skills that other kids picked up as easily as getting chalk dust on a sweater sleeve—reading, writing, and math—had become painfully difficult for her.

Janet began the third grade reasoning that perhaps her brain, like her hair, had grown out over the summer and she'd be able to learn like the other kids. But it hadn't. Within a few weeks she was asked by her teacher to stay after school for a bit of extra help. Just like last year.

Sitting up straight in a chair pulled up to the teacher's desk and clutching her pencil, Janet struggled to grasp the same lessons that the rest of the class breezed right through. Perhaps there was some trick to this, some method of operation that the other kids knew that she didn't. If only she could figure out their secrets! But no matter how Janet moved her head, squinted her eyes, shuffled the papers, she made little progress.

Every afternoon she'd try for a while and then begin to cry. Her teachers, baffled and dismayed by her lack of progress, tried and tried as well, but many days, after Janet had gone home, they broke down and cried too.

*Borderline IQ. Learning disabled.* The labels were applied in the middle of the fourth grade after Janet got tested. Not too much could be done for her, save a few marginally successful classroom modifications. Instead of being crushed, however, Janet was relieved. Discovering the facts about her brain made her life much easier. No longer did teachers pressure her—or themselves—so much. There were some things Janet could do, lots of things she never would. Most people, once they understood that, could live with it.

In high school Janet was assigned to special education classes. She finished the tenth grade reading and writing at about a sixth grade level and was able, if given enough time, to add and subtract most whole numbers. Core subjects like history weren't her favorites, but choir and home ec weren't so bad. Blessed with a pleasant disposition and a beautiful smile, Janet was well-liked at school and looked out for in the small town where she and I live.

When one day during her tenth-grade year Janet received a note requesting that she stop by the school guidance counselor's office after school, she wondered what it was about. Janet didn't think she was in trouble; at least she couldn't *recall* anything she'd done wrong. Still, one never knew, and Janet grew nervous as the afternoon wore on.

At 3:00 sharp the school counselor looked up to see Janet chewing her nails, shifting from foot to foot in the doorway.

"Hi there," the counselor greeted. "Come on in. Take a seat. Everything going all right for you?"

Janet relaxed. It didn't sound like she was in trouble. So far.

The counselor shuffled some papers. "I've been wondering about something, Janet. Would you be interested in studying cosmetology next year?"

Cosme . . . cosmeto . . . ? Janet struggled with the word. Hadn't she already had all her math?

The counselor clarified. "Would you like to learn to do hair?"

"Here? At school?"

"Right here. Starting next year we're going to offer three vocational classes to certain students. We'll have auto mechanics, building trades, and cosmetology. Are you interested?"

"Yes, ma'am!" Then a quick doubt. "Ma'am?"

"Yes?"

"You think I'm . . . I mean . . . do you think I can?"

"You can do this," the counselor smiled. "I'm sure of it."

The program, in fact, was designed especially for students like Janet—the kids who were not "college material" but who needed to learn a trade. All the classes would be small, allowing for lots of individual attention. Cosmetology would have only five students. The students would spend one third of their day in regular school and the rest of their time in vocational classes. Serious commitment was both necessary and expected, but if all went well, by the time they graduated, the students would have gained skills to help them earn a living.

All summer instead of dreading the beginning of school, Janet counted the days until school would begin. She bought hairstyle magazines at the drugstore, started studying the hairdos of every person she met, and began to dream about what it would be like to someday own her own shop.

Janet and her classmates found out that there was lots of stuff they had to learn before even being allowed to pick up a comb. Their instructor told them about hygeine and safety rules and how to care for their tools. They had to take tests and answer questions in class. This made Janet a little nervous, but the teacher, Mrs. Belle, was great. She went as slow as necessary for Janet and the other girls. If they needed to study and take a test over, that was fine with her.

When the girls finally got to pick up a scissors, they had so much fun. Working first on wigs and then on each other, Janet and her classmates practiced wet sets, finger curls, pin curls, and blow dries. They used curling irons and crimping irons, learned about scalp care and how to do a proper rinse. They even learned about setting up a properly organized station.

When Janet began her senior year in high school, she learned that on Wednesdays the class would offer free beauty services to anyone brave enough to call for an appointment. Although at first she was terribly nervous about working on "real customers," within a few weeks Janet came to love Wednesdays.

Mostly it was because she came to love Mrs. Beetles.

When news of the vocational programs appeared in the local newspaper, Mrs. Beetles pronounced that the idea of a beautician's course at the high school was simply wonderful. During lunch at the senior citizen's center, she told all her friends about it and bragged that she'd already called for an appointment. "Why no," she scoffed at her scaredy-cat friends, "I'm not a bit afraid they'll mess up my hair. Besides, those girls have got to learn don't they?"

Students were assigned to customers in the order that they'd called in, and on that first Wednesday, Janet got Mrs. Beetles. Although they'd never met before, the two of them hit it off so well that from then on Mrs. Beetles requested Janet every week. If "her girl" happened to be busy with another customer when she came in, well that was just fine. Mrs. Beetles didn't mind waiting one bit. And although she was down for a wash and set every week, most Wednesdays Mrs. Beetles left the shop the experimental subject of Janet's latest-learned beauty skill.

"Sure, honey, I'd love a manicure."

"Shape my brows? Will it hurt? Oh, go right ahead."

"Auburn? Well, I never thought about becoming a redhead, but let's try it."

"You're right. My face does look slimmer with contour cream. Even an old barn looks better with a fresh coat of paint!"

Folks at Mrs. Beetles' Wednesday-night prayer meeting never had to guess what the beauty-school girls were studying that week. Sporting fuchsia nails one Wednesday, shrimp-shaped eyebrows the next, and flaming auburn hair the week after that, Mrs. Beetles was a living, breathing, teased and sprayed visual aid week after week.

It wasn't just Janet's expertise that kept Mrs. Beetles coming back every week. During their appointments, Janet and Mrs. Beetles became good friends and chatted about all kinds of things.

"How's your dog? Is he still sick?" Janet would ask.

"You burned your hand on that curling iron again. Child! Did you put some aloe vera on it like I told you to?" Mrs. Beetles would say.

"I got a new swimsuit—it was on sale."

"Doc says I need to lose a few pounds."

"School's out in six weeks."

"My garden's coming up."

And one day late in May, "Mrs. Beetles, would you go with me when I take my state test? I'd really like it if you'd be my model."

How fun! Of course Mrs. Beetles would go. She'd be honored. It would be an adventure. She liked to travel—even if it was only four hours to Austin. Being a model sounded glamorous. "You never can tell," she teased. "I might end up on the cover of *People* magazine."

Mrs. Beetles was excited about the trip. So was Janet, but when the two of them boarded the big Greyhound the day before the test, Janet was so nervous she couldn't swallow.

She'd thought she was ready. Her teacher, Mrs. Belle, had said she was ready. But now she didn't feel ready at all.

As Janet stared out the window of the bus, she thought of all the tests she'd already failed. The math tests, the spelling tests, the history tests . . . Panic choked her so she could hardly breathe. If she didn't pass, it would be three months before she could test again. By then she surely would have forgotten all she'd learned in beauty school.

Mrs. Beetles' elbow in Janet's ribs broke the miserable train of thought. "You're looking pale, honey. Have some food." Hauling an enormous purse from the floor of the bus up onto her lap, Mrs. Beetles extracted a brown paper bag that looked like it had been recycled many times. Inside was some fried chicken and half a dozen bread and butter sandwiches with the crusts cut off. "Eat a bite. You'll feel better."

But Janet found it difficult to eat. "What if we can't find the place where we're supposed to go?"

"Map's right here."

Janet bit her nails. They might arrive late. The bus could have a wreck, or there might be a tornado.

"Honey, stop that. We're going to be just fine. This is fun. I haven't been to the capital in twenty years. And you've never been. Why, we are going to see us some sights!"

And they did, which helped to keep Janet's mind off her test. After checking into Motel 6 early in the afternoon, Mrs. Beetles sprang for a cab ride to the capitol building, and then they wandered around looking at other sights.

When it was dinnertime, Mrs. Beetles promised a rare treat. "I'm going to take you to a special dinner at a really fancy place. My sister took me there once, and I never forgot what a good time we had. I know you're going to like it."

Once inside the restaurant, Mrs. Beetles beamed with pride. "Isn't this grand? Food's good, too. Wait and see."

By the time they finished dinner and returned to the motel, Mrs. Beetles was chattering nonstop and having the time of her life. Janet began to feel a bit better. Perhaps things would go okay tomorrow after all. Maybe she *was* ready. Perhaps she *would* pass.

They watched television for awhile, then got ready for bed. Janet took off her glasses and set the alarm clock for 6:00 A.M. Mrs. Beetles put her teeth in a jar by the sink. They climbed into bed.

"Sweet dreams."

"Good night."

Mrs. Beetles began to snore.

Janet drifted off too and dreamed of shampoos and sets, but woke up dazed and dry-mouthed just after 3:00 A.M. She sat up, rubbed her eyes, and heard Mrs. Beetles vomiting in the bathroom.

Everything that happened after that was a blur. 911. Ambulance. Big whooshing automatic doors. Strange hospital. Pacing. Chewing nails.

Finally sweet words of relief from a doctor. "Your friend had an allergic reaction. It may have been something she ate; I understand she had seafood last night. We'll keep her here for a few days, but she's going to be fine."

"May I see her?"

Janet took one look and started to cry. Mrs. Beetles, resting on a gurney under blinding overhead lights, had a tube stuck up her nose and needles stuck into both arms. Without her false teeth—she'd left them in the room—her face looked mushy and soft.

"Honey, shhhh. I'm all right." She motioned Janet to her side. "I don't feel as bad as I look. Doctor says that I'm going to be fine. Listen to me. You go back to the room and get ready. Catch a cab to where you take your test. There's still time; you won't even be late. When you get there, find the

person in charge and tell them what happened. They can find you a model to take my place. I'm sure of it."

Then she threw up again.

Janet didn't get her beauty license. She didn't get it because she didn't pass the test. She didn't pass the test because instead of taking it, she stayed with Mrs. Beetles.

That was three months ago. Mrs. Beetles has completely recovered. But just to be on the safe side, she doesn't plan to eat shrimp ever again.

And Janet, who's going to try again to get her license, is planning a trip to Austin in a couple of days. Everyone knows it's going to be hard for her. Three months have passed, and the material is no longer fresh in her mind. Test-taking has never come easily for Janet, and there's a good chance that she will fail.

But when I think about how she stayed with her friend—even though it meant the possible end of her dream—it is clear to me that she's already passed the exam that matters most. In fact, I'd say Janet passed with flying colors.

You see, Janet may have a problem with her brain. But there's nothing wrong with her heart.

Nothing at all.

*Greater love has no one than this, that he lay down his life for his friends.*

JOHN 15:13

# ELEVEN

# Humble Pie

Last week I joined my two good gal pals Jeanette and Sheila for lunch at Luby's Cafeteria. It was girls' day out and the three of us were primed for good food and lively conversation. We planned to have lunch then hit several of our favorite antique shops.

While Sheila and I unloaded our trays of baked fish, broccoli, jalapeño cornbread and more, Jeanette showed us the pie she'd picked. Raving about it, she insisted that we each take a bite. It would be, Jeanette promised, the best, the richest, the most delicious dessert we'd ever put in our mouths.

No, it wouldn't do for us to wait until we'd finished our meals. We had to have a bite now. This, we were to understand, was not just pie.

Although she'd not seen it served in many years, Jeanette and this treat went way back. When she was a little girl, she would get dressed up and go downtown with her daddy to eat at Luby's once a month. They'd have a wonderful dinner together, just the two of them. No mother, no little brother, just Jeanette and her dad. After their meal, her dad would order coffee and they'd both enjoy a piece of pie—not just any pie mind you, but this particularly delicate, elegant kind. Remembering the special dinners she'd shared with her dad, Jeanette dreamily explained that this pie was like nothing else she had ever eaten.

Jeanette's dad is gone now, but before he passed away the two of them tried to identify the pie's unusual ingredients. They were sure that as good as it was, their special pie must contain some exotic ingredient, but they never did figure out what it was.

At Jeanette's urging, I forked a small nibble. Crumbly and rich, the pie was topped with vanilla-spiked whipped cream. Jeanette was right. It was scrumptious. Know what else? She was in luck, because I knew exactly what kind of pie this was.

"Ritz cracker," I told her. "It's called Ritz cracker pie. You make it with egg whites, sugar. . . . I've got the recipe somewhere at home."

Jeanette looked stricken. "Are you sure?"

I nodded and wiped my mouth.

"You mean all these years . . . all this time . . . what I thought was a fancy, exotic dessert was made out of *crackers*—the kind you buy at the 7–Eleven? The kind my kids eat with peanut butter?"

"But Jeanette," I interrupted. "It really *is* good."

"It is," Sheila agreed.

"Ritz crackers." She shook her head. "I don't even like Ritz crackers."

94

The phone rang.

"Annette Smith?"

"Yes. This is she."

"Do you have a minute?"

Sure I did. On the other end of the line was a woman from across the state asking if I would speak at her church's annual women's retreat. At the time I was just beginning to speak to large groups, and although I loved doing it, such requests caused my heart to pound and my palms to sweat.

Pretending a professional calmness that I didn't possess, I chatted with the woman while I checked my calendar. I told her that while I'd love to speak at her retreat, I had a few questions:

Did she want me to follow a certain theme?

How many sessions would best serve the group?

What were the ages of the women she expected to attend?

And finally, for curiosity's sake only, you understand, Who had given her my name?

Funny I should ask. Two Sundays ago during morning announcements, the minister said that the planning committee was seeking suggestions for that year's retreat speaker. Any woman who had a recommendation was asked to relay the appropriate information to one of the committee members.

As soon as the last amen was said, an out-of-town visitor—whose name no one caught—shared my name and phone number with one of the ladies. The woman was friendly and pretty, several members recalled, but she'd left quickly and no one knew who she was.

How interesting.

"She recommended you highly," the woman said.

Really?

"She could not say enough about how good you were."

Wow.

"In fact, the woman said that you were the best speaker she had heard in her entire life. We are just thrilled you can come."

Me too!

I hung up the phone and plopped down on the sofa, my mind going ninety miles an hour. The more I thought of the conversation, the more curious I became. Who could this mystery fan of mine be? I ran through a list of possibilities. No one I knew fit. *Perhaps she lives in San Antonio, where I spoke last fall. That has to be it. Someone from San Antonio. She'd have been traveling through town.* My thoughts flew. *I thought I'd done all right at the San Antonio retreat, but I guess my talks made a bigger impression than I realized. After all, if this unknown woman went out of her way to recommend me to a church she didn't even attend . . .* Tears filled my eyes. *I must have touched the woman's heart in a powerful way.* I wiped my eyes and let my mind jump ahead. *Maybe she's someone important, someone who plans those big Christian arena events. Perhaps she liked me so much that she'll give me a call. . . .*

My phone rang again.

"Mom!" I said. "I'm so glad it's you. You'll never believe what just happened."

Well, she just might.

"Isn't the whole thing too amazing?" I bragged when I finished telling her the story. "It's making me crazy, though, not knowing who gave them my name. I'd give anything to know who it was and how she knows me."

"Really? You want to know that badly who it was that told them about you?"

"Sure I do! I can't imagine who it could have been. Can you?"

Well, as a matter of fact, she could venture a guess.

"You're kidding." I could feel my overblown ego shrinking. "When were you at that church?"

"Two weeks ago. Your dad and I were up that way visiting friends. When I heard that they were looking for a speaker—"

"Mom," I interrupted, "you told those ladies that I was the best speaker you've ever heard in your life!"

"You are the best speaker I've ever heard."

"But you're my mother!"

"They don't know that."

And I was already booked.

Months later I did speak at the retreat, and the weekend was great. As always, I attempted to be transparent and open in my talks. The women responded to my efforts just as I had hoped—with laughter and tears, heartfelt prayers and hugs.

I suppose that while I was there I should have 'fessed up about my mother and all. But I didn't. It all seemed so complicated, and the event had gone so well. . . .

Truth is, I couldn't get up the nerve.

However, I learned a big lesson from that weekend. Now I realize that flattering words, like sweet desserts,

Perhaps, like Jeanette, you'll think this dessert is the best:

## RITZ CRACKER PIE

3 egg whites

1/2 teaspoon baking powder

1 1/2 teaspoon vanilla

1 cup sugar

20 finely crushed Ritz crackers

1 cup chopped pecans

2 cups whipped cream

1/4 teaspoon vanilla

Beat egg whites. When soft peaks form, add baking powder and vanilla. Continue beating, slowly adding sugar. Beat until stiff peaks form. Fold in crackers and pecans. Bake in well-buttered 9-inch pie pan at 350 degrees for 25-30 minutes. Let pie cool on wire rack. Top with a mixture of 2 cups whipped cream and 1/4 teaspoon vanilla and refrigerate until well chilled.

aren't always what they seem. And like Jeanette, I had some pie. It was humble pie, and I ate a great big piece.

*Know also that wisdom is sweet to your soul;*
*if you find it, there is a future hope for you.*

PROVERBS 24:14

# TWELVE

# Harlan's Ride to Fame

When eighty-three-year-old Harlan P. Whipple crashes his green 1979 Ford pickup truck into the drive-thru side of the town's only Dairy Queen, he doesn't understand what all the fuss is about. Leaning lightly on his cane, he stands to the side and studies the caved-in wall. It's not a very big hole, he thinks. Could've happened to anyone. Likely won't take more than a couple of two-by-fours and little dab of paint to repair the damage. Maybe a sheet or two of plywood. Not much more'n that.

Police Chief Todd, who Harlan suspects is plagued with constipation, has a different opinion when he arrives on the scene. He mops his brow and waves his arms around angrily, sweat rings reaching clear to his belt. "Harlan," he says, shaking his head, "you've gone and done it this time. What if little Jeanna Marie had been standing at the window, ready to take your order, instead of at the ice-cream machine making a malt? I'll tell you what. She'd have been killed!"

Harlan shakes his head. He is patient with the man. "Shoot, Chief, Jeanna Marie don't have to take down what I want to eat. She knows, don't you, honey? I eat the same thing ever' night that I live—Hunger Buster without tomatoes and pickles, and with extra cheese. By the way, do you eat much cheese, Sheriff?"

"Not the point, Harlan. It is not safe for you to be driving. You know it. Your kids know it. The whole town knows it! And I'll tell you what—I, for one, am through looking the other way. You are giving me your keys. Right now. I'm driving you home, and I'm calling Elizabeth and Harlan Jr. first thing in the morning."

One simple mistake of the feet—the gas pedal for the brake—was all it took for Harlan P. Whipple's driving days to end. Police Chief Todd made good on his threat. He didn't wait to cool down none, but called Harlan Jr. and Elizabeth the very next day.

Harlan cannot not believe it has come to this. His own son and daughter, not trusting their daddy's word that he would drive extra careful, came and sold his truck right out from under him. No longer can he hop in his truck and head downtown for toilet paper or dog food whenever he needs to. There won't be any more cheering up the old people down at the home on Thursday afternoons, no more hauling his own trash off, and no more nightly trips to the Dairy Queen. No more Hunger Busters.

"This stuff tastes like wet paper," Harlan complains to his chihuahua, Daisy. He's staring into a bowl of chicken and stars soup. "No substance to it a'tall. Kind of has a nasty whang to it. You wanna try some?"

Daisy turns her head.

"Don't blame you, sugar. It ain't no good." He pushes the bowl back. "What I wouldn't give for a Hunger Buster right now. Tomatoes and pickles—I wouldn't even care."

Harlan goes to the phone and dials 911. "Chief Todd there? No'm. No'm. I don't need an ambulance. Nor a fire truck neither."

He pulls off his cap and scratches his head.

"No'm, I'm not sick, but I do need to speak to the chief. Won't take but a minute of his time."

Daisy cocks her head to one side.

"Yes'm. I understand. I do, thank you."

Another moment's wait, then Chief Todd picks up the phone.

"Son," Harlan says sweetly, "reckon you or one of your boys could run down to the Dairy Queen and pick me up a bite to eat? I'll be glad to pay you for your trouble."

Folks around here rarely dial 911; they don't feel right about it. Unless something *really* bad is happening, people leave that number alone. But not Harlan. After he calls for Hunger Buster help three nights in a row—causing the poor dispatcher's blood pressure to shoot through the roof—Police Chief Todd concedes to a nightly routine. From now on at 5:00 sharp, one of the boys is to get in one of the town's two squad cars, go down to the Dairy Queen, pick up Harlan's Hunger Buster and tater tots, and take them to his house.

"Aww, Chief . . ."

"Quit your gripin', fellers," Chief Todd tells them. "You know as well as I do that now he's got started, Harlan's gonna call for his supper ever' night of his life. We may as well just go ahead and get it for him before he calls. If'n we don't, poor Annie's gonna have to retire. She can't be taking a 911 call ever' night now."

When the squad car arrives with his supper, Harlan is so obliged that he never fails to give the boys at least a quarter tip for their trouble. "Thank you, son. You want to come in? Aw'right. I understand. Maybe next time. Sure do appreciate it."

Harlan also tries to tip Mary Louise, the plump woman from church who comes every Monday morning to take him to the bank and the Piggly Wiggly. Harlan doesn't know it, but she's Chief Todd's favorite cousin. Mary Louise won't take the tip, but she does smile when, week after week, he slips a Snickers into her purse. Harlan thinks that a little weight looks good on a woman.

Folks are nice, they truly are. Harlan's kids come up every weekend to check on him. If he needs to go to the doctor, one of the neighbors takes him. If he runs out of toilet paper between Mondays, all he has to do is call and let someone know. He knows he has a lot to be grateful for. But still, not being able to drive is just about the worst thing in the world.

It is while listening to a morning show on the radio that Harlan comes up with a plan. According to the announcer, Sears is having a big sale. Washers and dryers, freezers, large appliances—all twenty percent off.

Harlan dials the phone.

"Does it ride pretty smooth? Got much speed?"

A pause.

"I understand. Yes. Real good. You boys deliver?"

Another pause.

"Mighty fine. Just one more thing, son. Could you fill the thing up with gas on your way? You can tell Fred to put it on my bill."

Harlan P. Whipple has just bought new wheels.

The sound of a honking horn causes Chief Todd to look up from the reports he's preparing. From his office window facing Main Street he can see that something is up. Although the police station is a good two blocks from the town's only stoplight, cars and trucks are backed up all the way to the station.

Could be a wreck or something, Chief Todd thinks as he heads out the door. Or maybe somebody's old junker has stalled out in the middle of the street. That'd be pretty likely. Then again, he wouldn't be surprised if he gets down there and finds that old Mrs. Tucker's goats have gotten out again, skittering around on the pavement like they did last week. He hopes not—he's too old and heavy a man to be out chasing livestock.

Once downtown, Chief Todd sees that there is no wreck. No one's car has stalled. No one's goats have escaped. But when Chief Todd sees what *is* causing the traffic jam, he sort of wishes they had.

For there is Harlan, traveling down Main Street toward the hardware store on a brand-new, super-sized, John Deere riding lawn mower. Traveling *dead center* down Main Street, as a matter of fact. Daisy is with him, barking her head off, standing up in a plastic, flower-decorated bicycle basket that Harlan has attached to the front of the mower with more than a dozen wire bread ties.

Harlan, who knows about the laws concerning motor scooters (a lawn mower is pretty close to a scooter, he thinks), has attempted to abide by the helmet law. Ever the law-abiding citizen, he is wearing a vintage 1950s football helmet, left from when Harlan Jr. played ball.

Smiling and waving, he is on the road again. But not for long.

It's not personal, explains Chief Todd. It's just that lawn mowers are not meant to be driven on public roadways. It's against the law. He doesn't write the laws; Harlan knows that. His job is to enforce them, and Harlan must not drive his lawn mower on the street.

Harlan looks at his feet, checks his fingernails. He doesn't hold anything against the chief. In fact, he feels sorry for the man, what with his stomach trouble and all. He doesn't want to cause the chief any trouble, doesn't want to be the cause of anyone's grief. It's just that a man's got to have a way to get around.

So Harlan still drives his lawn mower to town once or twice a week. But every time he sees, or thinks he sees, Chief Todd or one of the boys, Harlan turns into the closest driveway, pulls up into the yard, and pretends to be cutting folks' grass.

Watching Harlan on his route is pretty entertaining. He'll drive a half block or so, spot a squad car, pull up into a yard, and mow a round or two. Then he'll pull back onto the street, go fifty feet, back up into another yard, and so on. Folks on Harlan's route have gotten used to having odd strips of their grass cut unexpectedly.

Chief Todd knows what Harlan's up to, but, by George, the man is quick. Chief Todd has not yet been able to catch Harlan in the act. And one thing is for sure, there is no law against a man mowing someone else's grass.

One afternoon Harlan and Daisy run into something unexpected on their way to the Piggly Wiggly.

Daisy usually takes the rides in stride, especially now that Harlan has fixed up her basket with a little umbrella. She's very content with that little bit of shade and sits back on her haunches like she is the queen or something.

But on this particular excursion, Daisy senses that something is wrong. Harlan's mowing a path through the yard of the First Baptist church when she sits up yipping and barking, acting like she's going to jump out of her basket.

Harlan gears down and shuts off the engine. "What's the matter, sugar? What's got you riled up?"

Daisy keeps barking.

Maybe her stomach is upset. Harlan lifts her out of the basket, sets her on the ground. As soon as she's down, Daisy runs straight toward a bank of azaleas up against the east side of the church, still yipping away.

"Well I never . . ." Harlan gets off the mower and grabs his cane from where he's wedged it on the back. "Daisy! Girl! What are you after?"

Harlan limps to the spot where Daisy is barking. By now he can tell that she's upset at something in those bushes. Warily, he parts the leaves. *Oh my. It's Mary Louise. Parked right here under the azaleas.*

The woman is passed out cold.

"Diabetic. Didn't even know it."

"Doc says Mary Louise would have died if Harlan hadn't found her."

"I don't doubt it. And whatever would those three little girls of hers have done?"

"I hate to think."

Harlan is a hero. Folks all over town are talking about how he saved Mary Louise's life, how Daisy stayed with her while he went to the street and flagged down some help. If he hadn't been mowing across the church's lawn, if Daisy hadn't insisted on getting out of her basket—well, there is simply no telling how long the poor woman would have laid there.

"Harlan, I don't know how to thank you." Chief Todd weeps outside his cousin's hospital room. He remembers when he and Mary Louise were kids, how they swam together, rode horses together, skipped a lot of school together. Now Mary Louise and her husband play cards every Saturday night with Chief Todd and his wife. Their families take vacations together every summer, too.

After Harlan saved his cousin, Chief Todd found a loophole in the law that allows Harlan to drive his lawn mower on the outer edge of the streets—long as he stays at home during the busy times. "Guess it was there all along. Don't know how I missed it." The chief's voice is gruff.

Later that year, at the city council meeting, Chief Todd nominates Harlan to lead the Christmas parade down Main Street.

Harlan doesn't hesitate. Can Daisy come, too? Well yes, riding on a fire truck would be real fine. So would sharing a convertible with the homecoming queen. Which would he prefer? Well now that you speak of it, would it be just the same if he . . .

I can't help but smile as I stand here on the curb, watching as Harlan P. Whipple leads this year's Christmas parade. As I watch Harlan steer that John Deere, it comes to me that the whole town has learned something from Harlan the hero: When faced with a detour in the road, sometimes it's just best to cut a new path.

> *You have made known to me the path of life;*
> *you will fill me with joy in your presence.*
>
> PSALM 16:11

# THIRTEEN

# Angel on Aisle Seven

My sister-in-law Martha has a big sign hanging on the wall just outside her front door. It's colorful and cute, and I've seen others like it at craft fairs. The sign's message? A rural woman's theme: Gone to Wal-Mart. Be Back Soon!

Don't scoff. Going to Wal-Mart for many of us is more than a trip to purchase goods. It is a social event, a way to get ourselves out of the house. We're friends with the old man who greets us at the door. We share recipes with the ladies who check us out. The teenager who digs for our pictures behind the counter of the photo center is our neighbor's great-nephew.

Early in the morning in small-town stores across the country, groups of senior citizens gather in Wal-Mart snack shops. They come to gossip, drink coffee, and play Bingo. Although few of them care who wins, most players reluctantly turn in their cards when, after an hour or so of competition, the day's designated employee-turned-caller announces it's time to quit. She's needed in Domestics.

Well, all right, they understand. Once the game is over, players will sit long enough to finish their last cup of coffee before fanning out across the store to get whatever provisions they need (Metamucil and cat food are on most everyone's list). Once a month or so, they'll get a haircut or have the frames of their bifocals adjusted.

From ten until noon is the slow time at Wal-Mart, but come weekday afternoons, things pick up fast. That's the time when devoted but stir-crazy, stay-at-home moms appear at the entrance doors, leading their tousle-haired, just-up-from-a-nap offspring. Once the kids are safely caged in carts, the moms cruise up and down the aisles, checking out everything from birdfeeders to home décor. Best of all, the friendly salespeople provide these moms with some much-needed adult interaction.

No one at the store thinks anything of it when, after an hour or two of browsing, the moms end up at the checkout counter with only trial-sized bottles of Midol and half-eaten cans of Pringles. Store managers know that come hubby's payday, the moms will be back, checkbooks in hand.

On most evenings, Wal-Mart lobbies fill up with teenage boys who drink sodas from the machines and play video games. They're either waiting for their friends to get off work, or for their sisters, who take forever to buy highlighting kits for their hair. For the most part, the boys are well behaved. They may wander in to check out a CD or to go to the bathroom, but mostly they lean against the walls and watch the girls walk by.

And that's life at a small-town Wal-Mart.

One early spring afternoon we see Nathaniel Jones, whose wife died just six weeks ago, entering Wal-Mart. Although he has no written list, Nathaniel remembers what it is he needs—toilet paper, some motor oil, razor blades, and Velveeta cheese. Oh, and one last thing: flowers for Jeanie's grave. Tomorrow would have been her seventy-sixth birthday.

Aisle seven has a big selection of silk flowers. Too big for someone as sad as Nathaniel. Should he get red? Pink? Jeanie liked both. Roses? Carnations? He just can't decide.

"Hi."

Deep in thought, Nathaniel jumps at the sound of a voice from behind. He looks around. Oh. Only a little girl. She is a cutie, blonde, dimpled, smiling, and swinging her legs from the child's seat in her mother's cart, but Nathaniel ignores her. He pulls a stem of flowers from the store display, scratches his head, and wonders if they will fade. And how does one go about this? Should he get some kind of vase or just stick them in the ground?

Leaning toward him, the little girl says hi again—only this time a bit louder.

Nathaniel looks around. There is no one the child can be speaking to except for him. Her mother, whose back is turned, is standing several feet from her cart, chatting with a friend.

"What's your name?"

Nathaniel is surprised. Children don't usually take to him.

"Mmm. Nathaniel," he mutters gruffly.

"My name is Amy. I'm free."

"Free?" Nathaniel is confused. What is she talking about? Free kids? At Wal-Mart? He goes back to choosing flowers.

"See?" She holds up three fingers.

Nathaniel nods. Oh. Three. Of course.

How many stems should he get? *Two dollars each,* the sign says. Does that mean each flower or each stem? He looks around but doesn't see anyone to ask. Some of the stems have four, even five blooms on them. This worries him.

But the little girl hasn't finished her chat. She swings her legs and says, "Look. I have polish on my fingernails." Two dainty hands are lifted for his inspection.

"Nice. Uh, very nice." Nathaniel's jaw relaxes, and although he does not realize it, he is smiling for the first time since Jeanie died. He thinks he'll give the child a quarter so her mother can buy her some gum. Then again, what if she swallows it? Or chokes? He's heard of kids having to be cut open because they swallowed something they shouldn't. His best bet is to leave the child alone, pick out his flowers, and head on home.

But Amy isn't done with him yet.

"My shoe came off. Can you help me?" With complete confidence, the little girl hands him a white palm-sized sandal. It is a confusing contraption with about eighteen different straps and two buckles smaller than postage-stamps.

Nathaniel takes the shoe like he would a snake and wonders what exactly it is he should do. Mom is still chatting, totally unaware that her daughter has made friends with a total stranger. Nathaniel clears his throat several times, but she doesn't look around.

"Your mommy could help you," he suggests.

"No. You," she answers like a queen. Clearly he has been chosen for the job.

Okay. He'll do this real fast.

"That's the wrong way."

He tries again, but drops the little shoe and has to bend to pick it up. "Let's see . . . where does *this* strap go . . ."

Amy sits patiently while Nathaniel's knobby-knuckled fingers fumble with a buckle. He bends to the task, feels her warm hand as she pats his bald head. It tickles a bit. *When did children stop wearing sneakers?* he wonders. Shoelaces he

could do up with no problem, but all these buckles and straps
. . . well, they were confusing. Finally Nathaniel raises up.

"There now."

Amy peers into his face. "Thank you for fixing my shoe."

"You're welcome."

"I like you."

Oh, my. Nathaniel's face breaks into a grin.

"Sir? May I help you?"

Nathaniel turns to see a plump woman in a blue vest at
his side. Oh yes, the flowers.

"Yes, ma'am, you can," Nathaniel says as he looks at the
confusing display. "These flowers—are they priced by the
stem or by the bloom?"

"Let's see now. I believe it's by the stem. Yes. By the stem.
Two dollars apiece."

"Thank you." He picks out three bunches, then looks back
up to speak to his new little friend. He thinks he will give
the quarter to her mother. That will be safe. He bets she
likes gum.

But the child is gone. He looks up and down the aisles
for her cart.

"Sir?" The Wal-Mart lady is at his side again. "Is there
something else I can help you with?"

"The little girl in the cart, with her mother. Did you happen to see which way she went?"

"Excuse me?"

"Little girl. Blonde. She was right here. You walked right
past her."

The woman looks at him kind of funny and puts her hand
on his arm. "Mister, there *was* no one here. Just you and me
and these flowers. Nobody blonde, that's for sure. Now, I
always wondered what it would be like to be blonde. Thought
about dyeing my hair, but never could get up the nerve. Say,
how about we find you a vase to put those flowers in?"

Several weeks have passed, but the memory of the little girl in Wal-Mart still puts a smile on Nathaniel's face. No matter what he's doing, puttering around at home or sitting in his car at a stop sign, when he thinks about how she charmed him into helping her with her shoe, he breaks into a grin.

Curious how she disappeared so fast. Really curious that the Wal-Mart lady didn't see her at all. Isn't it?

I suppose there are any number of reasonable explanations as to what exactly happened that day. Perhaps the Wal-Mart worker overlooked the little girl. Maybe her mother was in a hurry to leave. It is even possible, I guess, that Nathaniel imagined the whole conversation and that she was never there at all. The man *is* seventy-eight years old, and I have it on record that he takes medication.

Truth is, you and I will never know. But from now on when I'm in Wal-Mart, cruising down aisle seven, I'll keep my eyes open for a little blonde girl wearing white sandals.

Just between you and me, I suspect she has wings.

*Do not forget to entertain strangers, for by so doing some people have entertained angels without knowing it.*

HEBREWS 13:2

# FOURTEEN

# Table Manners

I don't know anyone who likes to eat lunch alone. Breakfast? Sure. Many of us prefer to enjoy our first meal of the day in solitude. We need that time to shake off the sleepy-time cobwebs, to read the paper, and to meditate on our upcoming day. In the still of the early morning we enjoy what may be the quietest moments of our day. When you think about the kinds of foods we normally eat for breakfast, this makes sense. Oatmeal, Pop Tarts, or eggs are all what one might call "quiet" foods because they don't make much noise.

But when we eat our noon meal, most of us don't want quiet. We want company—someone with whom we can enjoy a nice noontime chat. Lunch is usually a social occasion. Girlfriends like to meet for lunch. Coworkers enjoy taking their midday meal in the break room with other employees. Even the busiest of stay-at-home moms is likely to sit down and eat lunch with her kids. The alternative, waiting until they're down for their naps, would definitely be calmer, but not nearly as fun. And a highlight of most grade-school children's lives is to have a parent come to school and eat cafeteria lunch with them.

But I don't believe that my grandma, Southern woman that she was, ever ate lunch. Mealtimes for her and my grand-dad—and they always ate four—consisted of breakfast, dinner, supper, and corn flakes or ice cream before they went to bed. No lunch. She served the big meal of the day at noon and called it dinner. Make no mistake, no matter what she called it, my grandma knew how to cook it. Anyone having dinner at her house would be treated to a bountiful offering of good country cooking. Along with at least one kind of meat (always fried), her table showcased various garden-grown vegetables, salads, home-canned pickles and relishes, cornbread, biscuits and butter, and desserts. Iced tea—sweet or unsweetened—was the beverage of choice for a meal at Grandma's house. Unless, of course, you were a kid. In that case you got milk—whether you liked it or not.

Anyone who ever sat at my grandma's table holds wonderful memories of her big noontime spreads. Those were times of great conversation, stories, and debates—for everyone but Grandma. Up and down she went during the meal, popping from her chair. Although we begged her to sit down and enjoy her food with the rest of us, she'd insist on getting up—maybe a dozen times during one meal—to fill our tea glasses, get extra napkins, or retrieve hot bread from the oven.

Once, in a comical attempt to *make* Grandma sit down, my dad, whom she called Sonny, tied her to a chair with her own apron—actually tied the strings into tight square knots! Never in my life have I seen a woman so miserable. She hollered and threatened, and even looked like she might cry. Although my dad was all of forty years old, if he hadn't let

Grandma go when he did, I believe she would have taken him to the back bedroom for a good whipping.

Unfortunately, memories of those tasty meals are all my family and I have left of dinners at Grandma's house. At ninety-two, Grandma's cooking days are over. Unable to care for herself, she now lives in a nursing home near my parents' place. It is a great blessing that Grandma has been content in her new home, due in part to the fact that both my parents keep a close eye on her care. By visiting frequently, meeting with the staff, and consulting with Grandma's physician, they do all they can to provide for her needs.

My dad, her only son and the child who lives the closest, is especially attentive to Grandma. He visits with her, pushes her outside in her wheelchair, and brings her vanilla milk shakes from the Dairy Queen. And mindful of how much Grandma has always enjoyed company with her meals, he shows up for lunch at the nursing home once or twice a week.

It's not as if Grandma eats alone—she shares a table with three other elderly folks. They eat in a cheerful, well-lit dining room, aided by well-trained nurses and aides. There is a lot of noise and activity going on during mealtimes, and she enjoys it all. But when my dad shows up at the dining-room table beside her—well, Grandma's face lights up with a joy that's reserved only for him.

"Sonny!" she always exclaims. "When did you get in?"

"Just now, Mother. How have you been?"

"Fine, fine. Pull up a chair. We're about to have some dinner. Won't you stay and eat a bite?"

She's always delighted when he says he will.

Last week, Dad made one of his noontime appearances at the nursing home. Grandma didn't know he was coming, but the kitchen folks did. He'd called ahead and asked them to set him a place.

"Hello, Mr. Woodall," an employee said when my dad arrived. (He's a familiar face, and the staff greets him by name.) "Your mother's looking good today. She'll be so glad you came."

Although it would be a little while before lunch was ready, Grandma was already in the dining room when Dad arrived. After their usual greetings, he poured them both a cup of coffee and sat down for a chat.

"Are you feeling good today? Is your sore toe any better?"

"Fine." Grandma's never been one to complain. "How's the weather outside today?"

"Supposed to turn cold. We need some rain."

Dad noticed a new face among the staff. "Mother," he asked, "is that little girl one of the new dining-room aides?"

"She is. Her name's Patricia, and she seems real sweet."

As Dad and Grandma talked, residents of the home began to drift in. Some hobbled in on their own, some used canes and walkers, and others in wheelchairs, like Grandma, were pushed in. Before long the room was full, bustling with chatter and activity as the workers hurriedly served the residents. They poured tea, milk, and juice and made sure all were in their seats, so that when the trays were brought out everyone would be ready to dive in.

As they waited for their lunch, Dad noticed that Grandma's coffee was getting low. "Would you like more coffee, Mother? I'll get—" Dad stopped talking midsentence as something funny was laid across his neck. He reached up to see what it was and felt his hand being gently pushed away.

Dad heard a soothing voice coming from behind him. It was the new aide, Patricia. "Sir, it's time for us to eat. That's your napkin. You need to wear it while you eat. Please, now, let's don't pull it off."

Dad looked down, and discovered that, like everyone else in the room, he had been "bibbed"—draped and tied with one of the adult-sized bibs that the staff respectfully referred to as "napkins." First he turned red and then he began to laugh.

Poor Patricia then realized what she had done. "Oh, oh," she said, trying to get the words out. "I'm so sorry! I didn't see your face and I thought you were ..." She snatched the bath-towel-sized garment from around his neck, stood beside him, and twisted the cloth in her hands.

"Louie Woodall," my dad said, standing to shake her hand. "Patricia? Nice to meet you. No harm done. You know I *do* get a bit messy when I eat, but if it's all the same," he winked, "I think I'll pass on my bib today."

To be honest, I doubt that my grandma realized exactly what was going on. But, oh, how I wish she did! After all the teasing and joking and silly shenanigans my dad has put her through, she would have gotten the biggest kick out of the whole thing. She would have told all her friends and neighbors about how her Sonny got bibbed.

But I've been thinking; since Grandma can't spread the tale, can't use the story to get back at him, maybe I will.

Yes, indeed, I think I will.

> *Even to your old age and gray hairs*
> *I am he, I am he who will sustain you.*
> *I have made you and I will carry you;*
> *I will sustain you and I will rescue you.*

ISAIAH 46:4

FIFTEEN

# *Holy Haircut*

For the past several summers Randy and I have directed small church groups on weeklong medical mission trips to Mexico. We travel to areas of dire poverty and set up temporary clinics, offering free medical and dental care in the name of Christ. The home churches fund the trips and pay for things like the free medicine and dental supplies we dispense. The church also pays the travel and lodging expenses.

Our job as leaders is to prepare team members for what they will face once they get to Mexico. We answer questions and talk about what to pack, how to dress, what the food and accommodations will be like. We let them know that since we work in cooperation with Mexican doctors, dentists, and ministers, it is important that everyone who joins a team be prepared to follow our hosts' directions once we arrive in Mexico. We also spend a great deal of time discussing cultural differences and our need to respect and blend in with the people we go to serve. Team members hear lots of do's and don'ts: Don't feed the dogs. Don't wear shorts. Do respect the differences in men's and women's roles. Don't assume someone doesn't speak English. Do eat what is put before you. Do smile. Do learn to say *gracias,* and do slow down.

Shortly after one such trip, Randy, my daughter, Rachel, and I left the little church where we'd worshiped for five years. We decided to begin serving with a larger congregation, one that offered more activities for teens. It was a difficult choice, but one we made after more than a year of thought and prayer.

A bit weary and—right or wrong—looking to take a break from mission-team leading, Randy and I planned to slip quietly into a pew and behave ourselves. Neither of us wished for attention, nor did we seek ministry leadership roles. We planned to be pleasant pew potatoes for at least a good year.

Right. (Was that the Father's chuckle I heard?)

Within weeks of making the move to the new church, folks learned of our past involvement in Mexico missions. "Tell us about it," they said. "We want to hear all about it." "What good work!" "When can our church go to Mexico?"

Randy and I gazed helplessly at each other. Here we go again. Are we ready for this? They really wanted to make a trip? Really? After all, our new Christian family hardly knew us. We hardly knew *them.*

Apparently they knew us well enough.

Mission trips to Mexico are expensive, we explained. Very expensive. Did the church have the several thousand dollars necessary to fund such a trip? Sure it did. Several wealthy members had declared they'd make up the difference if the church budget couldn't absorb the entire cost.

Summers are busy, we reminded them. What with vacations and other commitments, would there be enough people willing to go? Enough? More than twenty eager-beaver, Bible-toting believers showed up for the first informational meeting, raring to go.

We made a last attempt. There was scheduling to consider. We would need to work around church youth camp, community outreach day camp, Vacation Bible School, and other summer activities. Not to worry. It was all worked out, church leaders told us. See the calendar? The first week of July, which was totally blank, would be the perfect time for a trip.

In the face of such generosity, optimism, and opportunity, what real choice does a pair of reluctant team leaders have? None! This past July, Randy, Rachel, and I, and our fourteen new church friends packed up and set out for Mexico.

Folks often ask just what it is that we do when we go to Mexico. Do we preach? No. Teach? Not exactly.

What then?

Although our goal on every trip is to share the love of Christ with the people we serve, the manner in which we do so is different every time.

One thing that is always the same is that tons of children come to the clinics with their parents. Like kiddos everywhere, these beautiful, brown-skinned darlings love attention. Although shy at first, they warm up after a bit. Team members always find ways to break the ice. Bridgette painted the little girls' fingernails and played ball with the boys. Leigh Ann and Rachel tied hair ribbons, blew bubbles, and dispensed miles of stickers and a bucket of gum. Connie, Deanna, Debbie, and Beverly set up a makeshift Sunday school room utilizing wooden church pews. They dispensed crayons, glitter and glue, tiny watercolor paint sets, along with lots of coloring-book pictures of Jesus.

In other corners of the church building, two Mexican doctors listened to patients' ailments, then dispensed advice, free medicine, and gentle invitations to attend the evening's worship service. Out in the sunshine, a handsome young Mexican dentist stood all day, pulling tooth after bad tooth from the mouths of grateful patients. I took patients' blood pressures while they waited their turn.

Randy, Rick, Jake, Jamie, Hugh, Andy, and Aric piled into the bed of a local cowboy's pickup truck. They were driven to the outskirts of town to the homes and farms of people who owned livestock. These seven—a math teacher, a volleyball coach, a preacher, and four high-school students—would serve as amateur veterinarians for the week. They had brought worming medicine, which is a simple treatment but unaffordable to these folks, with them from Texas. Worming medicine makes the animals, which their owners depend on for food and meager income, healthier, stronger, and more productive. Under the blazing sun, dozens of sheep, goats, cows, pigs, and donkeys were roped, wrestled, or chased through cactus, mud, and manure and given measured doses of the free treatment.

One team member performed a service unique to this particular mission trip. Kathryn, an energetic grandmother of two of the teen members of our team, arrived in Mexico toting not glitter or glue, hair ribbons or gum. She carted neither worm medicine nor a blood-pressure cuff. Kathryn came all the way to Mexico carrying a little blue suitcase containing an assortment of combs, clips, scissors, and plastic capes. Kathryn came to Mexico to do what she does best: give haircuts.

Lots of haircuts.

Kathryn was one popular lady. While the rest of us experienced lulls in our work, she stayed busy from the time the clinic opened until the end of the day when we were ready to go back to our hotel. Hour after hour, working in extreme heat and near one hundred percent humidity, she bent over men, women, and children, clipping, cutting, and trimming. Although she spoke no Spanish and most customers spoke no English, Kathryn kept a running dialogue going all day long.

"Shorter?" she'd motion with her hands.

"Above your ears?"

"Bangs?"

"Do you like it? Yes?"

With her outgoing personality, wide smile, and frequent bouts of laughter, Kathryn was a hit. She teased the women, tickled the children, and made the men hold their heads just so. When a customer had lice-infested locks, she didn't flinch, but just went on cutting. Only after the person was well out of sight did she methodically spray her equipment with a disinfecting solution. She gave each person their own comb to take home from a box of more than a hundred she'd brought with her.

I'm sure Kathryn's back hurt. I watched her feet swell and saw sweat run into her eyes. But I didn't hear her complain. Concerned that she might overdo it and have a heat stroke or something, I made her sit down every few hours, put her feet up, and drink some water. Left on her own, she likely wouldn't have stopped for a minute.

It was late in the afternoon on the last day of our trip when we watched a man and a woman trudge up the hill toward the clinic. I greeted the pair, learned they were mother and son, and found them a seat where they could catch their breath and wait.

Did they need to see a doctor?

No.

Perhaps the dentist?

Not today. They'd come for the friendly *gringa*—the one who cut hair. "My son," the mother explained to me (I speak a little Spanish), "his hair, you see it is much too long." Her arthritic hand reached up and stroked the man's scraggly hair, then flicked lint from the shoulder of his white shirt and carefully straightened his collar.

He sat beside her with his head down, unusually slack-jawed and soft-shouldered, and undisturbed by his mother's ministrations. Not until he lifted his head and I saw his face did I understand. The woman's son had Down's syndrome.

This twenty-five-year-old man, she explained, was her only child.

I fought back the unexpected tears that welled up in my eyes. *How hard life must be for the two of them,* I thought. Mexico is a country that provides no pensions or social security, one in which the elderly depend on grown children for income and care. This woman was still the one giving care, and no doubt she would be providing for this son as long as she lived.

While I fought back tears, Kathryn sprang into action. Sure she could cut his hair, any way his mom wanted it done. She took the man's two hands in her own and held him steady as she moved him toward the hair-cutting chair. Once he'd sat down, she slipped the cape over his shoulders and began to gently comb his hair, careful not to frighten or startle him. His mother stood nearby, ready to soothe him should he start to fight or cry.

She needn't have worried. The man didn't cry. He didn't whimper and he didn't flinch. Tentatively at first, then with more confidence, Kathryn began to cut, first the front, then the back and the sides, a little snip here and a little snip there. As she worked I observed her whisper in his ear, stroke his cheeks, and touch his chin. Those of us sitting nearby watched in wonder as she charmed him.

So comfortable was the man with Kathryn that before she was finished cutting, he had fallen asleep in the chair. His arms hung down and his ear rested against Kathryn's own heart. She seemed not to mind the man's head on her chest, but simply worked around his sleeping face as best she could. When she finished, Kathryn brushed away the hair, cradled the man's sleeping head in her hands, and smiled up at his mother.

"What do you think? Short enough?"

One expects to encounter holiness in church—to sense it in the filtered light of stained-glass windows, to hear it in the strains of great hymns and in public prayers offered by well-spoken men and women. One does not expect to find holiness in a free haircut.

But that is exactly what I found.

*"If anyone wants to be first, he must be the very last, and the servant of all."*

MARK 9:35

# SIXTEEN

# The Bribe

"Whatcha looking at?" my husband, Randy, questioned.

"Nothing much. Just scanning." Although my nose was buried in the Sunday employment section of the newspaper, I kept my answer deliberately vague. "You know. Seeing what's out there."

"I thought you liked it at the hospital."

"I do."

"Anything interesting?"

"Maybe."

It is clear to me that some people look upon the fact that I change jobs every couple of years as a sign of instability, maybe even of incompetence. I promise it's not. I'm a dependable employee and folks are generally sorry to see me go. (I've evidence of that fact—I have a shoe box crammed full of "We're Going to Miss You" cards.) It's just that I'm easily bored and

I look forward to change. Being a writer, a speaker, and a registered nurse, I've found that there's always something new for me to try.

On this particular day, the following ad caught my eye:

HELP WANTED:
RN needed to work at therapeutic
wilderness camp for troubled teens.
Remote location. Part-time hours.
Apply in person.

Work with teenagers? At a camp? In a remote location? How interesting.

I have to admit that on the morning of my interview, I questioned the wisdom of my pursuit. The facility was located less than ten miles from my house. Easy commute, had been my first thought. But I found out that seven of those miles were down a narrow, winding, rutted dirt road. I bumped and slid, dodged three deer and a fox, and after the first mile and a half, stopped seeing any signs of modern life. This place really was remote. Should I commit to making such a drive every day?

But then I toured the camp and met some of the kids, and every doubt dissolved. I wanted this job. Badly. And seeing as how I was the only nurse to apply, I got it.

Working at the camp was unlike anything I'd done before. My patients, the kids at the camp, ranged in age from twelve to seventeen. All of them had emotional and behavioral problems. They'd been abused and neglected, or had been arrested or were on drugs. They were sweet and sad, conniving and cute. It was my job to address their health-care needs, monitor their medications, assess and check them, and make necessary referrals. I did all that and a little bit more. For although not a requirement for the job, I fell in love with them on my very first day.

I loved the staff, too. I was struck by how young the workers were; most were college graduates in their mid to late twenties. For weeks I couldn't tell the kids from the staff. But they endeared themselves to me with their creativity, their originality, and their spunk. Sure, they dressed funny and they talked funny, but they challenged my assumptions and nudged my slightly older brain toward more innovative thought.

Even my boss, Melanie, the camp director (who, I recall, wore overalls to my interview), was not yet thirty years old. It startled me to find someone her age assigned to such an important position. How could she handle the responsibility of running the camp? Did she know what she was doing?

She did. Studious and smart, and within months of getting her master's degree in counseling, Melanie was energetic, innovative, and dedicated. She directed the camp with compassion, creativity, and a high degree of professionalism. Gifted with grace and maturity, she dealt with the myriad problems and challenges present in such a setting with a poise and insight beyond her years.

It was easy for me to forget that she was twenty-seven years old.

However, one situation, or should I say one child, almost got the better of Melanie. I'll call him Shaun. Charming and manipulative, this thirteen-year-old was not doing well in the program. Shaun had trouble getting along with peers, had been kicked out of three different schools, and had started running away from home at the age of nine. He needed one-on-one attention. It was decided that Melanie, soon to be a licensed counselor, would carve specific time from her schedule to meet with Shaun.

Week after week I watched as she prepared for their sessions. She'd review Shaun's file and go over her notes from their previous meetings. What had she tried last week? What could she try different this week? I saw her doing extra reading, and I know she made calls to a former professor, seeking his advice and counsel.

All that preparation should have helped. It didn't.

Shaun was a master at controlling the situation around him. If Melanie tried to talk about his relationships with peers, he would launch into a philosophical discussion about the controversial lyrics of a favorite rap group. When she broached the subject of his failure in school, he would pick up objects from her desk and offer to teach her to juggle. Once when she proposed playing a fun communication game, he took up the entire hour improvising ways to improve on the game's rules.

"We'll play next week," he assured her. "Okay?"

It wasn't that Shaun couldn't cooperate, just that he chose not to. Perhaps he reasoned that if he made only microscopic progress, his sessions with Melanie would go on forever. I am convinced that the two hours a week of undivided attention he received from her were the highlight of his stay at the camp.

Melanie did not exactly share his enthusiasm.

"You'll see me on Friday?" As always before leaving Melanie's office, Shaun extorted a commitment for their next session.

"Same time. And please try during these next few days to think about some of the things we discussed." Melanie spoke through gritted teeth.

One day she stumbled into my office and flopped down on the couch.

"Tough session," I surmised.

"You could say that."

"Wouldn't sit still?"

"Nope."

"Wouldn't stay on the subject?"

"No . . . not at first . . ." I saw her eyes drop.

"Excuse me?"

"I bribed him. He was bouncing off the walls, and my head was hurting, and I totally lost it. I broke every rule in the book."

"Big deal," I soothed. "Don't be so hard on yourself. You reached your limit. Happens to everyone. No harm done. Besides, what did you offer him—a soda?"

"No."

"Candy?"

"No."

"Extra phone call?"

She shook her head.

I'd run out of guesses. "What then?"

Melanie shifted in her seat, chewed on a fingernail, and suddenly looked every bit her age. "I told him if he'd behave appropriately for ten minutes, I'd let him . . ."

"Let him *what?*"

"See my tattoo."

See her tattoo! Deep breath. Do not act shocked. This is not the time or the place to be judgmental.

"You have a tattoo?" I asked in what I hoped was an even voice.

"Three." She blew her nose.

"And they would be . . ." I became acutely aware of every one of my forty-plus years.

"My newest one's on my ankle. That's the one he asked to see."

Only a cough betrayed my relief. "Your ankle. Can *I* see it?"

She pulled down her sock. Sure enough. Mickey Mouse. Right there on her ankle.

"Nice" was all I could think of to say.

Several months ago Melanie left the camp to take a promising position at a larger facility across the state. It was a difficult decision for her, but the choice she made was a good one. I stayed home the day of her going-away party. What can I say? I'm a wimp and I know it. It's easy enough when *I'm* the one doing the leaving, but it breaks my heart when I'm left behind, and I couldn't bear to tell my friend good-bye.

On my first day back to work after Melanie had gone, I found on my desk a gift she'd left for me. It was the size of my fist, unusually heavy, and wrapped in plain white tissue. Inside the paper I found an iridescent, crackled glass ball, capped at the top with intricately carved silver, suspended by a gossamer ribbon. It was one of the loveliest, most delicate things I'd ever seen.

I held it to the light and read the handwritten words Melanie had enclosed:

> This ball, beautiful despite all of its cracks and flaws, is a symbol of the kids we serve here at camp. They come to us broken and cracked, but through love and care, the beauty that is inside each of them—and in us—begins to shine through. Take care.
> Love always,
> Melanie

I recalled the day I'd been shocked to learn that she had a tattoo, and my remembered reaction brought a smile to my face. The glass ball reinforced what Melanie had been teaching me all along: You shouldn't judge a person by their outward appearance—even if they do have tattoos.

Thanks for the lesson, Melanie.

But by the way, dear, you aren't planning on getting any-thing pierced—are you?

*Man looks at the outward appearance, but the LORD looks at the heart.*

1 SAMUEL 16:7

## SEVENTEEN

# Will the Yolk Be Unbroken?

Summer vacation at Uncle Louie and Aunt Marolyn's Texas cattle ranch was the best. Out of his mom and dad's cautious sight, six-year-old Robert could be as rowdy and get as dirty as he pleased. At the ranch he could ride horses, fish for crawdads in the creek, play in the hay barn, and pretty often skip his bath.

During the rest of the year, Robert lived with his parents in an urban area of Minnesota. A soft-spoken, good-natured sort of boy, he behaved in the mannerly, civilized way that his mannerly, civilized parents expected him to. He took piano lessons, chewed with his mouth closed, hung his bath towel up right, and always flossed before bed.

But during Robert's time at the ranch, Aunt Marolyn didn't care if he left his bed unmade. Clothes that matched weren't a big deal to her, and she let it slide if he left vegetables on his plate. At some meals Aunt Marolyn didn't even serve vegetables. Unless, of course, you count gravy.

Uncle Louie let Robert ride everywhere in the back of his pickup truck, just as long as he sat down. In the morning they fed the cows, and in the afternoon they went to the feed store or the cattle-auction barn. It was at the auction barn that Robert learned that grown men could spit.

When his week at the ranch was over, Robert flew home to Minnesota all by himself. His parents arrived at the airport a full hour early. They waited and paced, and paced and waited, nearly wild in their eagerness to see him. However, when their brown-eyed son first came into view, the sight of him was so startling that for a moment, neither of them could manage a word.

Their dear little Robert, whom they'd sent to Texas wearing creased cotton shorts, a department-store shirt, white canvas sneakers, and folded-down socks, tumbled off the airplane clad in hand-me-down blue jeans with rips in the knees, shiny red cowboy boots, and one of Uncle Louie's old crushed straw hats. From the pocket of his snap-up western shirt bulged an empty chewing-tobacco pouch, placed there for effect. Clasped in his hand like a spear—almost as long as he was tall—was a bleached rib bone of a dead cow.

"Howdy y'all," Robert greeted them with hugs. "Look what I found in the pasture, Mom. Uncle Louie said I could keep it!"

After the initial shock wore off (watching your kid cart a cow bone across the tarmac would likely inspire even the most indulgent of moms and dads to stop and take stock), Robert's parents realized that no harm had been done to their clean-cut little boy. It was with their blessing that during the following summers he made more short visits to the ranch.

When Robert turned sixteen he concocted a great plan and sold it to his parents: He'd go to Texas and stay all summer. Not just to have a good time, but to work for Uncle Louie for money. It would be great.

Uncle Louie agreed; he was all for a boy pulling himself up by his bootstraps and becoming a real man. "Shoot, we'd be glad to have you. But Robert, you aren't a kid anymore. If you're coming to work for me, I'll expect you to really work. Is that understood?"

"Yes, sir."

"Won't be a lot of goofing off."

"I want to work, Uncle Louie."

But Louie knew teenagers.

On the first morning after his arrival, Uncle Louie woke Robert up early. At 5:30 to be exact. "Time to get up. Rise and shine. Out of bed. NOW. Breakfast in ten."

"Yes, sir."

Robert sat up, rubbed his eyes, and looked incredulously at the clock. He didn't know anyone who got up this early.

Two whole minutes passed before Uncle Louie hollered up the stairs again. "I SAID get up. Breakfast is ready!"

Robert jumped into his clothes, pulled on his work boots, and bounded down to the kitchen. Uncle Louie, who preferred to cook his own morning meal, had their plates full and on the table. Breakfast consisted of two fried eggs, three biscuits, and a pile of bacon, cooked real crisp.

"Milk?"

"Please."

"Orange juice?"

"Sure."

Robert dove in. Man! Uncle Louie was an awesome cook.

While he chewed his eggs, Uncle Louie outlined Robert's summer work schedule. There were cows to be fed every day, fences to be painted, and hay to be cut, raked, baled, and brought in. Robert was expected to work every day until noon, come in for an hour or so for lunch, then finish up in the afternoon.

"Take a water jug with you when you leave this morning," Louie ordered. "One's there by the sink. And don't let me see you working without some kind of hat."

Robert was a good kid and a hard worker. He tried hard to do exactly what Uncle Louie asked him to do. But he *was* only sixteen. Like any teenager, Robert forgot stuff. He did things wrong. He got distracted. Sometimes he goofed off.

Uncle Louie made things clear over the morning eggs. "Robert, next time I want you to be *sure* you get the gate closed."

"Yes, sir."

"And it cost a lot of time when you let the tractor run out of gas in the middle of the meadow. Hay's gotta come in today, before it rains. This morning check the gas gauge before you get started."

"I will Uncle Louie."

"And Robert . . ."

"Yes?"

"Do you want another egg?"

On some mornings Robert felt like his crusty uncle was glad he was around. He'd whistle while he cooked, tell a story or two, and have a second cup of coffee before heading out to work. Other mornings, silent and preoccupied, Uncle Louie would put Robert's plate of eggs on the table with little more than a grunt. Those days, Robert wondered if he'd done something wrong.

Uncle Louie's morning moods might be warm or cold, depending on how things were going. But one thing about him never changed: The man could make the best fried eggs in the world. Robert ate them every single day that summer. Soft centers, firm whites, not too greasy, but crispy around the edges—there was no contest. Uncle Louie's eggs were the best that Robert had ever put in his mouth.

It was at the end of that summer, after the hay was in and the fence was painted, that Robert finally asked, "Uncle Louie, could you teach me to cook eggs like these?"

"Why sure I could," Uncle Louie answered. "Matter of fact, I could eat another egg myself."

They went to the kitchen.

"Get you a big heavy skillet and about a quarter inch of grease. Turn your fire on high and get your grease real hot. Hand me that hot pad, will you? Now you drop your eggs in real easylike. You can cook more than one at a time, but try not to let them touch."

"You cook the eggs on just one side?"

"Nope. You gotta flip 'em. Watch real close. When the center starts to get firm, you slip your turner under your eggs, one at a time. Be real careful. Just ease 'em over in the grease, like this. See? Aww shoot!"

"What's the matter?"

"Broke the yolk. After all the eggs I've cooked, don't know why I can't turn 'em without breaking 'em. I end up breaking about one out of six."

"What happens when you break a yolk?"

"Whole egg turns hard as rubber. It's no good."

"So you throw out the ones you break?"

"Nah. That'd be a waste. You eat 'em."

Funny. Robert couldn't remember eating a rubbery egg. Not one all summer.

The next morning he took notice of the two breakfast plates Uncle Louie made. His plate held two eggs. Both had perfect centers. Uncle Louie's plate had one egg cooked right and, sure enough, one with a broken yolk.

The next day it was the same.

On the third day, both of Uncle Louie's egg yolks were broken.

Robert said nothing, but kept on noticing. On most mornings at least one broken-yolked egg made it to the table. Never did such an egg make it to Robert's plate. Not even one.

Go figure.

Robert is a grown man now—thirty-something years old with a wife and a son. The three of them live in the city, and Robert likes it there. I know, however, that he fondly remembers those weeks spent in the country on Uncle Louie's ranch.

How do I know? Well, he's my cousin and he told me so.

Robert wants his baby boy, Cort, to experience the same kind of work and fun that he enjoyed. He'll wait until Cort's a bit older, of course, but then he'll send him to the ranch. If it's okay with Louie.

There's one thing Robert will explain to Cort before he goes, the thing that he learned a long time ago. Uncle Louie can seem kind of stern, a bit gruff sometimes. There'll be days when Cort may wonder if Uncle Louie's glad he's there.

"Son, there's no need to wonder," his dad, Robert, will say. "There's a sure way to tell that Uncle Louie really cares. It's all in the skillet."

*Your love has given me great joy and encouragement.*

PHILEMON 7

Part 3

*Unto Us
a Child Is Born*

EIGHTEEN

# A Toothy Mistake

If they held Olympic games for mothers, I'm afraid that my friend Hope would not win the gold medal. Don't get me wrong; Hope's a devoted single parent and loves her kids. She's got two of them, a darling six-year-old named Heather and an energetic four-year-old named Mike. Like a ferocious mother lion she would go to the ends of the earth to protect them; that is, if she was able to remember where she parked her car.

Hope is, politely put, organizationally challenged. She forgets things like Halloween and haircut appointments and what time school lets out. But because she's funny and sweet and would do anything for her friends—if she could remember where we all live—we are glad to help out.

When Hope forgets to pick Mike up from T-ball, we wait with him at the park and call her on our cell phones. Fibbing that we're on the way to pick up our sons, we manage to remind her to come get her own. When she signs up to bring dessert to the potluck, we pick up an extra cake, just in case she forgot. And when Hope gets herself into a tearful mess trying to sew a costume for a school play or attempting to wallpaper her den, we drop what we're doing and help her.

But there are some things Hope has to manage for herself, like visits from Santa or the Easter bunny. Or the tooth fairy.

I bumped into Hope's daughter, Heather, at a school play last night. "Hi sweetie! How are you?"

"I lost my tooth. See?"

She had indeed. "My goodness. Did the tooth fairy come to see you? Did she leave anything under your pillow?"

"Yes ma'am, she did. Twenty"—I thought she'd say cents—"whole dollars."

Twenty dollars? Since when was that the going rate? Since when was Hope rolling around in such dough?

I found out the truth when I saw Hope later that night. The loss of Heather's tooth had been quite exciting, Hope told me. She had taken lots of pictures and put the tooth in a special envelope with the date recorded on it, so she would never forget the day Heather lost her first tooth.

I was impressed. But that wasn't all.

In an absolute frenzy over the possibility of a supernatural visit, Heather had insisted on washing, drying, and curling her hair before bed so she'd be sure to look pretty for the tooth fairy. Then she'd brushed her teeth, cleaned up her room, and pulled her newest nightgown on over her head. The whole thing had been quite a production.

But twenty dollars? There was more to this story.

After all that tooth-fairy prep work, Heather was so worked up that she couldn't go to sleep. Indulgently, Hope read her three stories, rubbed her back, and sang her half a dozen songs.

Heather did not get sleepy. But Hope did. It was almost 11:00.

Ever the understanding mom, Hope brought Heather a glass of water, tucked her in tightly, and read one more story.

Heather remained wide awake. It was going on 11:15.

By now an extremely tired mom, Hope got tough. Leaving the room, she told Heather she'd have to go it alone. No discussion. No arguing. Good night. If she didn't go to sleep, the tooth fairy might not come!

After closing Heather's door, Hope stumbled around the house, started the dishwasher, locked all the doors, and turned out the lights. Finally, she put a movie in the VCR, curled up on the couch, and settled in to wait Heather out.

It was a long wait. Hope fell asleep on the couch.

At 3:30 in the morning Hope woke up to see the test pattern on the TV. Disoriented, she pulled herself to her feet, rubbed her eyes, and tried to remember what it was she'd forgotten.

It came to her. The tooth fairy! Of course. Not daring to turn on a light, Hope groped for her purse, dug out a dollar, and tiptoed to where her daughter slept. Gently, smoothly, she traded the tooth for the dollar bill, then crept to her room and crawled into bed.

No surprise, bright and early the next morning an exuberant Heather danced into Hope's bedroom, waving a bill in her hand.

"Mommy, Mommy! Look what I got!"

Hope sat up in bed and pulled Heather up beside her. "Wow, you must be a very good girl. You got a whole . . ." Hope's mouth fell open. Heather wasn't waving a dollar, nor a five, nor a ten. Heather was holding up a twenty dollar bill.

"I meant to give her a one." Hope related to me. "But it was dark, and by mistake . . ."

I stifled a giggle.

"Annette," she placed her hand on my arm, "this is serious. Heather has *four more* loose teeth!"

Oh my.

I know Hope doesn't want to hear this, but she'd better get ready. This only marks the beginning. Parents spend an inordinate amount of their children's growing-up years groping around in the dark. Like Hope, they fish around for one thing, come up with another, and all too often give their kids something different than what they planned.

"Cheer up," I managed to say.

She looked at me quizzically.

I gave my friend a wink and a hug. "Haven't you heard? Only the first tooth merits a twenty. After that, it's just a quarter apiece."

*Wisdom is found in those who take advice.*

PROVERBS 13:10

# NINETEEN

# Ruben's Choice

Grandma Sadie and Ruben go back a long way, way back to when Grandma learned of Ruben's existence at the same time as his own mother, Judy.

It is a Tuesday morning. Sadie and Judy are sitting at Sadie's kitchen table. Sunlight streams in through the window over the sink, and Regis and Kathie Lee chatter on the TV in the den. Outside a dog barks and Scooter, the cat, wails to be let in. There is coffee and toast, although neither of them feels like eating.

Sadie attempts to stay calm while Judy, who is fifteen days late, teeters on the verge of a meltdown.

"Pink, I'm pregnant. Blue, I'm not," chants Judy. "Pink. Blue. Pink. Blue. I am. I'm not. I am. I'm not. Oh please, oh please, let it be pink." She looks at her watch, suddenly thinks a terrible thought, and begins to wring her hands. "Mother, what if I counted wrong? What if I did the test wrong? What if it doesn't work?"

Sadie fears the same. In her day, a woman depended on a doctor for news like this. Home pregnancy tests bought at the grocery store? She can't help but wonder. Sadie feigns a confidence she doesn't feel.

"Relax, honey. If you can't tell for sure, well you'll just take the test again."

One minute passes. Then another. Sadie fiddles with her toast. "How much time now, honey?"

"Eleven minutes." Judy looks at her watch. "No, ten and a half. No. No. Ten. Ten more minutes is all."

After what feels like hours, the timer in the kitchen sounds and the two of them race to the bathroom where the test results wait on the edge of the tub. Both bend to get a look.

Pink.

The test is pink!

Judy races to the phone and calls her husband.

Baby Ruben is on his way.

It's another sunny Tuesday, and Ruben and Grandma Sadie are driving to the zoo. He's four years old and his parents are now divorced. But being with his best pal Grandma really helps Ruben.

"Grandma?"

"Yes, Ruben?"

"Why do birds eat worms?"

Grandma ponders his question but knows she's unlikely to come up with an answer before he asks her another question.

"Grandma, how come I can't see the moon when it's light outside?"

Sadie should have paid better attention in school.

She changes lanes and checks the rearview mirror, stalling for time while she thinks. "Well, Ruben, honey, it's like this," she begins. But then a dog darts across her lane. A big German shepherd. Where did *he* come from? She grips the steering wheel, feels a thud, and realizes to her horror that the front corner of her van has made contact with the dog. She looks to the side just in time to see the ragged bundle of fur tumble across the pavement like an empty cardboard box. Sadie can't believe what just happened.

"Grandma!" Ruben shrieks from the back seat. "What was that?"

Sadie makes a U-turn and steers back to where she hit the dog. He was a big one, but if she can get the poor fellow up into the back of the van, there's a veterinarian's office just up the street. Perhaps she'll flag down someone to help.

When they get to the spot, Sadie carefully pulls over on the road's shoulder, and she and Ruben get out. The area is overgrown and it's difficult to see, but she thinks the dog must be somewhere in the area.

"Ruben," she cautions as they part the weeds, "when we find the dog, I want you to stay back. When animals are hurt, sometimes they bite."

But when the two of them finally stumble onto the animal, yards from the road, Sadie can see that he's dead. Tears fill her eyes and she tries to shield Ruben from the gruesome sight, but he twists away from her and manages a look.

Sadie worries about the effect that seeing the terrible accident will have on Ruben. His reaction does not seem normal to her; once they climb back into the van, he does not speak of the dog, does not utter a single word about it.

And so as planned, although Sadie's heart is not in it, they drive on to the zoo, where Ruben runs and plays and makes silly faces and noises in front of the monkey cages. The two of them go to McDonald's for lunch, where he gobbles down his Happy Meal and a good part of her Big Mac. He chats nonstop about preschool, his best friend Mike, and even explains to her why french fries taste better if you eat them with your eyes closed.

Sadie follows his lead, not mentioning the dog, but frets just the same. Hitting the poor animal has been a traumatic experience for her. It *has* to have bothered Ruben, too. Keeping feelings bottled up is not a good thing. *Reader's Digest* says that, and Sadie believes it. Ruben should talk about what he saw; Sadie is sure of it.

Hours pass. It is evening and the two of them are sitting on the front porch swing, waiting for Ruben's mom to pick him up and take him home. Back and forth, slow and smooth, the swing sways. The mood is hypnotic, and Sadie feels Ruben relax against her side. This is a good time. She'll talk of it now.

"You know, Ruben, it makes me very sad that the dog got killed today."

He says nothing, just stares at some spot on the porch.

Sadie's heart is breaking. She racks her brain for words to say, gropes about for a phrase to comfort the child.

"You know, honey, I think that pretty dog is up in heaven with God, right now."

Ruben raises his head.

Grandma Sadie, who knows her Bible, is stepping out onto some pretty thin theological ice. She knows it, but she simply does not care. She pulls her grandson close and strokes the top of his head.

"Ruben honey, I believe God wanted a dog just like that for himself."

Ruben doesn't respond for a little while. He shifts and fidgets, then leans back again. Sadie can see that the little guy is deep in thought. They swing some more. Finally Ruben sits up and pulls away from her. Head cocked to one side, eyes dark and serious, he looks up at her.

"Grandma?"

"Yes, sweetheart?"

"What's God going to do with an old dead dog?"

Grandma Sadie isn't the only one who thinks Ruben is smart as a whip. His teachers think so, too. By the time he's in the second grade, he's doing fifth-grade math and devouring young-reader chapter books. Ruben likes *The Boxcar Children,* but the *Hank the Cowdog* series is his all-time favorite. He's yet to read *Old Yeller,* but he loves the movie so much that he's seen it eight times.

Ruben likes to read about cows and horses and dogs, but when he gets home from school every day, it is Mavis the cat who greets him. Wearing a red bandana that she can't seem to get rid of, Mavis rubs on his legs, purrs loudly, and meows for him to pour her fresh food.

"You've already got food, Mavis," Ruben chides each time. "Okay, okay, just a little."

People think that only dogs are smart and can learn tricks. Ruben knows better. When he whistles three times, Mavis—no matter where she is in the apartment—scampers to the kitchen and pounces up onto a low wooden stool. When Ruben says to her one of the few Spanish phrases he knows—*buenos días*—Mavis lifts her paw for a good morning shake. When he leaves for school he calls, *"Adiós gata"*— good-bye cat.

"Meow," Mavis answers.

As far as Ruben can tell, no one else at his school has a cat that can speak Spanish even half as good as Mavis can.

When Mavis first acts sick, Ruben's mother, Judy, doesn't think it's anything to worry about. Cats, like children, frequently pick up colds. As a general rule, they get better on their own, with a bit of TLC.

Not this time.

A week passes and Mavis is truly ill. She's listless and lazy, eats less and less, and drinks very little water. It is when Mavis misses greeting Ruben at the door—snores right through his homecoming—that Judy thinks that something is seriously wrong. The next day while Ruben is in school, she brings Mavis to the vet.

The news is bad. Mavis has feline leukemia, which is treatable but not curable. It is also very expensive. "It would be best," advises the vet, "to spare both your suffering and hers by putting Mavis to sleep real soon. She's only going to get worse. I can promise you that."

When Ruben and Judy are eating dinner that night, she breaks the sad news to Ruben. He doesn't believe her at first.

"But Mom, Mavis doesn't look real sick. What if she's just tired?"

Judy tries to explain. "Ruben, Mavis *is* sick. She's not going to get well."

"Are you sure?"

"Yes. The vet said that Mavis is hurting. We don't want her to be in pain, to suffer. Even though we want her to stay alive, it would be mean and selfish of us to keep Mavis alive when the best thing, the kind thing, is to have her put down."

"Put down?"

"That's what you call it when you put an animal to sleep. Remember Old Yeller?"

"Oh."

Three days later Ruben is talked into the right thing. He cries when they take her but tries to be brave. He knows that Mavis should not be made to suffer, but it still hurts.

They bury Mavis in Grandma Sadie's backyard.

Grandma Sadie has been chronically ill for more years than anyone would guess. Not one to favor sackcloth or ashes, even on the days that she feels rotten, Sadie gets herself up and dressed, puts on her makeup, and fixes her hair. When she's feeling very sick, she takes special care to dress in bright colors and to wear eye-catching jewelry and a snazzy shade of lipstick.

Judy is aware of her mother's illness and understands that despite Sadie's peppy appearance, she's incredibly fragile. But that's all she knows. Judy learned a long time ago that there is no point in asking her mother for lab-test results and doctors' prognoses. Sadie will not give them.

"No, I don't want to talk about it. I'm fine. I do not intend to become an old woman who sits around and expounds on her ailments to anyone who will listen. I mean it. I'm not discussing this with you."

Being kept in the dark does not keep Judy from worrying. She sees the puffiness around her mother's eyes, the big purple bruises on her arms, and watches how the veins in her neck pulse wildly when she climbs the porch steps. She knows that Sadie, who's always loved dresses, is wearing pants today, not, as she insists, because it may turn cold, but because they hide her swollen ankles and feet.

By sheer determination, Sadie has lived an active life for longer than is expected of folks with her condition. She has managed, up until now, to hang on to the tiniest smidgen of health she has left.

Until now.

Precipitated by no specific event, the effects of Sadie's disease rush upon her like a tidal wave. Multiple organs show signs of failure, first the liver, then the kidneys, and finally the heart and lungs. Medicine that has worked in the past isn't effective anymore. Neither lipstick, blush, nor bright clothing will provide relief today.

Sadie is dying.

Judy and Ruben, twelve now, drive home from the hospital after visiting Grandma Sadie.

"Mom?"

"What, sweetie?"

"Is Grandma getting better?"

She keeps her eyes on the road. "No, Ruben, I'm afraid she's not."

"Will Grandma ever get to go home?"

"No, honey. She's not going home."

Ruben is silent for a moment, then asks, "Is Grandma going to die?"

Judy swallows. "Yes, Ruben. Grandma is going to die."

Then Ruben gets around to asking the really hard question. "Is Grandma in pain, Mom? Is she suffering?" He sounds like a grown-up man.

Judy hedges, wanting to say no. She keeps her eyes fixed on some spot up ahead in the road. "I'm not sure, honey. The nurses are giving her lots of medicine to make her feel better, but it doesn't seem to be working as well as they hoped."

Finally Judy pulls into the driveway and they unbuckle their seatbelts. Judy starts to get out, then notices that Ruben isn't moving. She turns to him. His eyes are dark and serious and he's trying to be brave.

"Mom," he says, "I've been thinkin'. Maybe we ought to put Grandma down."

"Excuse me?"

His face is earnest. "Should we put her down, Mom? You know, if she's suffering. Like Mavis."

"Oh, honey." Judy pulls him to her chest. For three days she's fought the urge to cry, but now, unbelievably, she finds herself fighting back laughter.

She tries not to snort and takes gulps of air. Like the good mother she is, Judy controls herself long enough to explain to Ruben the difference between the care given to cats and to people, and he is terribly relieved.

"Are you as sick of casseroles as I am?" Judy asks out of the blue.

He is indeed, for the neighbors have been very, very good.

"How about we go get a pizza for supper? Rent a movie, too."

Ruben thinks his mother's idea is great, so they buckle back up.

Judy knows already what kind of pizza they'll get—pepperoni and black olive. She knows too what kind of film they'll see. Ruben will want something funny; he always does.

Shocking, some might say. Pizza and a movie? With your dear mother and grandmother on her deathbed? Surely not! But Judy doesn't care. There'll be time enough for tears tomorrow. Tonight they will laugh.

Sadie would approve.

> *Weeping may endure for a night, but joy cometh in the morning.*
>
> PSALM 30:5 KJV

155

# TWENTY

# Trash to Treasure

On the ledge over my kitchen sink, I nurture ceramic pots of herbs and ivy. In my flowerbed I plant petunias in the spring, mums in the fall.

Not my friend Christie. She cultivates shallow tubs of surly looking miniature cactuses in her kitchen and has pulled up all the grass in her side yard to plant what reminds me of a miniature Death Valley.

"Look at this one," Christie croons over a cactus. "Isn't it cute? Have you ever seen such a gorgeous flower?"

*Or such long thorns?* I think to myself.

Christie frequently spends long weekends and most of her vacations tromping around under a hot desert sun, collecting rocks and poking at things with sticks. She comes home tired and sunburned, telling crazy tales about snakes and scorpions and two-day hikes. She can't explain the desert's appeal; it's like something out there calls her name.

The beach exerts a similar pull on me. Nowhere am I as peaceful as beside the sea. The sound of the waves soothes me; the smell of the air energizes me. When my seat is in the sand and my feet are in the surf, all is well with my soul. My dream is someday to live in a house that looks out on the ocean.

Randy loves the water, too. Since our children were small, we've spent most of our vacations in Destin, Florida. We rent a small condo within walking distance of the shore, and besides sleeping and visiting our favorite seafood restaurants, we spend every moment on the sand or in the sea. It is for all of us one of the best weeks of the year.

Only our first visit to the shore was disappointing.

Russell, eight years old, and Rachel, four, had no idea what to expect, but they were excited. I'd primed them for fun with new swimsuits and flip-flops, plastic buckets and shovels, towels and swim masks. I promised them we'd go swimming every day, build fancy sandcastles, and if they were very good, I'd help them bury their daddy deep in the sand. And, I told them dreamily, we would collect lots of seashells— maybe even starfish and sand dollars. I pictured the four of us strolling the shore at sunrise, picking and choosing from a beach littered with a dazzling array of shells.

There was only one problem. When we got to the beach there were no shells to be found. None. I questioned the manager of the condominium and learned that just being at the ocean was not a guarantee that there would be seashells. Truth be told, we could expect to find few, if any, shells on this particular beach. However, she helpfully informed, if we cared to drive a few hours down the coast, we could increase our chances of successful hunting.

But we'd already driven hours and hours and would have to do the same to get back home. We decided that it was not worth spending any more of our precious vacation time on the road, not even to collect shells.

Unfortunately, I'd built this up big.

"Mom, I promised my friends I'd bring them some back."

"How come there aren't any shells? You said we'd get to pick the prettiest ones."

"I wanted a sand dollar."

"I wanted a starfish."

Out of earshot of the children, Randy and I decided that on the last day of our trip, once we were packed and headed toward home, we'd surprise the two of them with a stop at a souvenir shop. We realized that buying shells from a store wouldn't be the same as spending a morning combing the beach, but it would be better than nothing. At least, we reasoned, the kids would have something to show their friends.

The week passed way too quickly. On the last night of our stay, Randy decided to treat us all to dinner at a special seaside restaurant. Captain Dave's was a bit pricier than the eateries we'd sampled so far, but it offered excellent fresh fish and a breathtaking elevated view of the water. We'd heard from other vacationers that it was not unusual to spot dolphins on the surface of the water below.

The establishment lived up to its reputation. Our meal was delicious, and we were delighted to observe a group of dolphins cavorting just yards from where we dined. The evening ended perfectly with a gorgeous, flame-colored sunset over the ocean.

The four of us were reluctant to head back to the condominium, especially Russell and Rachel. Stalling, they asked if they could take just one last swim. A short one? It wasn't completely dark yet. If not a swim, then could we maybe walk on the beach for a little while? Please?

"Sure," Randy agreed. "We can walk for a half hour or so. Then we'll have to go back and start to pack up."

I slipped my hand into his, and the two of us followed a few yards behind as the two of them scampered their way down the steep, sandy path that ran from the back door of Captain Dave's down to the water.

"Hey!" we heard Russell exclaim. "Look at this."

"Oh, Mommy, come look at what we found."

The two of them came running back up the path toward us, holding something in their hands.

"What do you have?" It was dark where we stood.

"Shells!"

"There's a whole bunch of 'em."

"Aren't they pretty?"

"Come look!" they said as they pulled us with them.

Randy and I stood speechless at the foot of their find. They'd found shells all right, a huge pile of them. Hundreds maybe. And not just any shells, mind you, but oyster half shells discarded from the restaurant, perhaps by Captain Dave himself.

"I found a big one."

"I found a double one."

"This one's pretty."

"There *are* shells on this beach. You were wrong, Mom."

And so I was. Oblivious to the fact that the shells they'd discovered were really garbage, the two of them filled their pockets and my purse, and made plans to share the plunder with their friends.

Twelve years have passed. Russell is now twenty, Rachel sixteen. Families—and vacations—change. This summer when we went to the beach, Russell stayed home to work and Rachel brought along her friend Lauren. We spent the week swimming and sunning and walking on the beach, and no one even cared that we didn't find any shells.

No matter. I still have an oyster shell from that first trip. A couple of years ago when preparing to move to a new house, I found a shoe box full of them in the back of Rachel's closet. They'd been tossed aside, forgotten and no longer valued. I tucked one single shell into the front pocket of my jeans and tossed the box into the trash.

From where I sit this morning, I can see that shell resting on a low shelf, a single remnant of long ago treasure. Every once in awhile I pick the thing up and hold it in my hand. This specimen, the one I chose to keep, looks pretty much like all the others we collected that night. It's gray and bumpy on the outside, plain and smooth on the inside. It's not very pretty, and even after a bleach and a water soak, the thing still carries a musty odor.

But I keep it, because when I hold it in my hand, I'm taken back to a starlit night when my children taught me something about value. It's a secret kids know by heart.

Treasures are everywhere. It's all in knowing how and where to look.

Happy hunting!

*And a little child will lead them.*

ISAIAH 11:6

# TWENTY ONE

# *Light on the Subject*

The religious tract rack, conveniently located in the back foyer of Lucy Owen's childhood church, provided a bountiful supply of fresh reading material for her and her fifth-grade friends. The rack was mounted so high on the wall that when they were younger they'd not even realized it was there. Only when they reached the second grade did they begin to ponder what exactly those brightly colored pages were, and they longed to get them in their hands. However, at that age they were tall enough to see the tantalizing rack but not tall enough to reach it.

Could they have asked their parents to get them a tract? I suppose. But they didn't. None of them cared to hear the dreaded parental refrain: *Those are for grownups, not for kids.* They could wait.

Sometime after Promotion Sunday (several of the girls had hit their growth spurt by then), it became routine for one or more of the fifth graders to pilfer a tract every week. Past the age of coloring books and Cheerios, they were allowed to sit together down in front, apart from their parents, *if* they were good. Under the watchful eyes of a dozen or so mothers, they'd stealthily pass the paper contraband up and down the pew during sermons.

"Got a tract?" whispered one without moving her jaw.

"Lemme see it when you get through."

"I'm after her."

With their cartoonlike illustrations and catchy titles, the tracts provided easy-reading relief from the tedium of what the preadolescents deemed extremely long sermons.

Some of the tracts interested them more than others. "How to Become a Christian," "Evolution—Fact or Fiction," and "The Submissive Wife" were okay. But "Should Women Wear Pants?" and "Why Men with Long Hair Are Displeasing to God," both of which contained lots of exclamation points and entire paragraphs typed in capital letters, were better.

Lucy's favorite tracts were the ones about sin. Head down, she read all about smoking, drinking, gambling, even lust and adultery, in detail. Laced with personal testimonies about people whose lives had been ruined by such sins, the tracts scared Lucy. She took their words as gospel. Especially convicting to her soft heart was the teen-targeted tract titled "Why Christians Can't Dance." It chronicled the life of one foolhardy girl who, after attending her very first dance, became pregnant, dropped out of school, and had to get married. Fifth-grader Lucy wasn't sure how it all took place, but since she did not want such a thing to ever happen to her, she vowed then and there that she would never, ever, dance. Not in the sixth grade. Not in the seventh grade. Not even in the eighth.

Piously unswayed by some of the kids in youth group (even the preacher's daughter; can you believe it?) Lucy refused to dance—even when she went to high school. One might assume that her social life was stunted. Not so. In spite of the fact that every time dancing broke out at an otherwise wholesome event, she insisted on leaving, Lucy never lacked for dates. The boys she went out with were such sweethearts that they acted with complete understanding about the whole thing.

Take for instance the junior prom. When Lucy explained to her escort that because of her religion, she couldn't dance, he was more than willing to leave after the meal. While other, less convicted, girls stayed inside the gym and danced, Lucy and her date were in the parking lot.

Necking.

She was, after all, a girl of stalwart beliefs.

Lucy, now the married mother of two teenage girls, is a friend of mine. Since I have a daughter too, we compare notes about this parenting stuff. Lucy and I remember our teen years well, which is likely why we have grown extremely nervous that our girls have started to date. Crazed might best describe what we've become.

Neither of us can bring ourselves to say—you know—that *word,* so we speak in code. Have we done a good job teaching our daughters about *pancakes?* Have we prepared them to deal appropriately with their desire for *pancakes?* What in the world would we do if either of us found out our daughters were experimenting with *pancakes!* On more than one occasion, we have become so upset just talking about *pancakes* that we were forced to make an emergency trip to IHOP to make ourselves feel better.

Last year, sixteenth birthdays loomed in the near future for two of our girls. Being the sensible, sane mothers we pretend to be, Lucy and I calmly set up some rules for our daughters.

No dating before sixteen.

Home by midnight.

All potential dates must meet our approval before they can take our girls out.

We (and their dads) have absolute veto power.

Lucy added one additional rule for her girls. She does not like it when they sit out in the driveway in the car once they've arrived home from their dates. ("Can't imagine why," I tease her with a smirk. "Think they might get out of the car and start dancing or something?") As their curfew approaches, Lucy posts herself at her kitchen window, which faces the front of her house. When a daughter and date pull into the driveway, she notes the exact time on her watch. After ten minutes, if her daughter hasn't come in, she politely flips the porch light off and on. This is a prearranged signal that means "Get into the house, NOW!"

After flipping the light switch that first time, Lucy watches to see if her daughter comes in. If she doesn't after five minutes, Lucy flips the porch light on and off again, twice this time.

If the offending daughter is still outside sitting in the car, Lucy will stand at the switch and flip the light off and on, off and on, off and on. Nonstop. As long as it takes, which isn't very long.

Lucy's plan has worked great up until just lately. It seems that for the past month or so, her front-porch lightbulb has been burning out almost every week. She'll go to flip the switch on a daughter and her date, only to find the light burned out. This will occur in spite of the fact that only hours before, when she checked it, the thing was working fine.

"Cheap bulbs. Stop buying those off-brand lightbulbs," I advised. "Get the good kind. Spring for the extra twenty cents. It'll pay off."

She took my advice, but it didn't help. The name-brand bulbs burned out just as fast as the cheap ones.

"Fluorescent. It's the only way to go," said the hardware store man. "They're pricey to begin with, but outlast regular bulbs ten to one."

They didn't.

A fuse problem, maybe?

Nope. "Fuses check out fine," assured the electrician.

I suppose Lucy would have never figured out the problem and would have just taken to buying lightbulbs by the case, had I not pulled up in her driveway one evening as her daughters were leaving on their dates. The two girls, flanked by good-looking boyfriends, emerged from the front door and stepped out onto the porch just as I drove up. They were laughing and talking and took no notice of me.

*They're so pretty,* I mused as I watched from my car, *and growing up so fast. How is it that our babies have become such beautiful young women? They're such sweet girls, both of them. . . .*

So lost was I in thought that I almost missed what happened next.

In a well-practiced move that didn't cause him to miss a step, one of the girls' boyfriends reached up and gave the porch lightbulb a quick, loosening turn. So nonchalant was his action that the girls didn't even notice.

I realized with a smile that between the two couples, someone had been responsible for unscrewing Lucy's porch lightbulb every Saturday night for going on a month!

Now, I know that if I was the friend I claim to be, I'd have gotten out of my car, hauled all four kids back into the house and made them 'fess up to Lucy. It would have been the right thing to do. But those sneaky kids were so cute that I simply couldn't bring myself to tell on them.

Until now that is.

Sorry, girls.

Sorry, guys.

Lucy? Don't be mad. Look at it this way. At least they weren't dancing!

*But everything exposed by the light becomes visible.*

EPHESIANS 5:13

# TWENTY-TWO

# Her Wasn't There

Cherry Baker never did figure out exactly how it was her garage roof caught on fire. True, she had been burning leaves in the backyard. The blaze had ended up just a bit bigger than she intended, and there had been the teeniest of breezes that day.

Still, it was an awful shock to look up and see the shingled roof on fire. She had tried to put the flames out with the water hose but got scared and ran into the house to dial 911. Local firefighters had arrived in an instant, so all that got damaged was the roof and one side of the garage.

After that incident Cherry decided to do two things for the rest of her life. She would bag, rather than burn, her fall leaves, and every Tuesday she would deliver homemade coffee cakes to the men and women on duty at the fire station. Cherry Baker's cinnamon-pecan coffee cakes were so good that rarely did a firefighter miss a Tuesday shift.

From the fire station, Cherry drove to the Easy Living Rest Home near the edge of town. That's where her Aunt Gonzie lived. The nurses and aides at the small facility took wonderful care of Aunt Gonzie. They saw to it that she and the other residents had whatever it was they needed to be content and comfortable, be it a fresh nightgown, the day-room TV tuned to a favorite soap opera, or as in Aunt Gonzie's case, a midday dip of snuff.

Cherry appreciated their efforts, and so she did her part to make the place more pleasant. Several times a year, wearing a big straw hat, knee pads, and flower-print cotton gloves, Cherry drove to the home. Her baby-blue Chevrolet station wagon always rode low on those occasions, not, as a suspicious patrolman once guessed, because she was smuggling liquor into this, a dry county, but because of the buckets and buckets of compost, bags of pine-bark mulch, gardening tools, and bedding plants loaded in the back.

The gardening would take her the better part of a day, but by the time she was finished, the courtyard flowerbed—onto which all of the resident's rooms opened out—would be filled with colorful annuals. There'd be petunias, verbenas, salvia, marigolds, and begonias during the warm months, and bronze and gold mums, and yellow and purple pansies when it turned cold.

"What do you think, Aunt Gonzie?" Cherry would wipe dirt from her gloves, rear back on her heels. "Do these beds look all right?"

"Real pretty, sugar-foot," Aunt Gonzie would say. "You've got it looking nice today."

Along with gardening, Cherry liked to shop. Folks at the Wal-Mart were accustomed to the sight of her pawing through the sale racks, scouring for bargains on everything from dish towels and laundry soap to house shoes, hair dye, and size 3X ladies' underwear. None of it was for her, mind you—

she bought it for the local battered-women's shelter. Those gals needed all the help they could get, Cherry knew. If she could pick up a few things every week, well, every little bit helped, didn't it?

Thirty years before, Cherry had landed a starring role in her junior college's production of *Guys and Dolls.* Because of that fact, she was the closest thing to a theater expert her little town had. And so every year, for more than ten years, she volunteered to help with the high school's play. Since the school had no real theater sponsor, if it wasn't for Cherry, they probably wouldn't have had a production.

She had great fun with the kids. They worked really hard to put on a great show, and so did Cherry. She helped build sets, sewed costumes, and painted promotional posters. One year when the kids did *The Music Man,* a key student musician called in sick on opening night. That evening Cherry ended up not directing from the wings but down in the orchestra pit, playing third trumpet. It had been awhile since she'd blown a horn, but she did her best, and it wasn't too bad.

On Mondays Cherry helped deliver Meals on Wheels, and on Wednesdays she kept the nursery for the young mothers' Bible class at her church. Saturdays were grandkid slumber-party nights, and on Sundays Cherry cooked a big after-church lunch for all three daughters and their families.

"Do you work full-time or part-time?" a telephone surveyor once asked Cherry.

"Why, neither," she answered. "I don't work at all." Scouts honor; that's what she said.

Cherry's husband, George, admitted to mixed feelings about his wife's busy pace. On the one hand, he was glad she was happy doing all her projects. But on the other hand ("Can you get me a glass of iced tea, hon? Another piece of peach pie?"), he sometimes worried that she did too much.

171

Truth is, George didn't even attempt to keep up with Cherry. "Nursery day?" he would ask over eggs.

"Nope. Nursery's Wednesday. Today's Monday. Meals on Wheels. But I'll be home by 2:00."

"Right. I remember now," he pretends. "Have fun. Drive careful. Don't be running any old people down in the Meal a Day van." Then George pecks Cherry on the lips and gives her rear a squeeze. He'll see her this evening, maybe take her out to eat.

It was in the evening, after just such an ordinary Monday, that George came home to the unexpected sight of Cherry asleep. Not dozing on the couch, but curled up on the bed. Only 5:30 and his wife was in bed?

"Honey?" he called.

She didn't stir.

"HONEY?" Something wasn't right.

George called for an ambulance.

Once they got to the hospital, Cherry was whisked out of sight, and long minutes passed before anyone came out to talk to George. The news was not good. Doctors were puzzled, not sure what was wrong. It was an infection of some kind, and it was unusually aggressive; had she really been okay up until today?

So quickly did Cherry's condition deteriorate that within hours nurses whisked her from a regular hospital room to the ICU. Shocking even the most pessimistic of doctors, Cherry died unexpectedly on Wednesday afternoon.

Everyone reeled in shock and disbelief. This could not be. On Monday morning life was fine, but today—a mere two days later—George's wife and the girls' mother was gone? Impossible.

Cherry had so many people who loved her that her funeral was packed. By the time the service started, cars were parked everywhere, including three fire trucks, their drivers on call.

Inside the church, every pew was filled. Those attending included members of the high-school drama class, who, unaccustomed to death, sat with pale faces, biting their nails. Residents of Easy Living Rest Home were near the front, some of them clutching just-plucked flower bouquets. Brave women from the battered-women's shelter, many of them wearing clothing donated by Cherry, wept quietly in their seats near the walls.

After the service, folks rallied to help. Not only was enough food brought in to feed a small army—eight loaves of banana bread, five casseroles, and four Jell-O salads—but attentive friends, neighbors, and church members took care of a myriad of behind the scenes details.

One person, noting receipts on the kitchen counter, picked up Cherry's dry cleaning. Another friend took three rolls of Cherry's film to be developed at Photo Mart. Someone else went to sit with Aunt Gonzie. Arrangements were made for alternate volunteers to cover Cherry's day delivering hot meals and to keep the nursery for the young mothers' class.

Folks did their best to fill in the gaps left by Cherry's death. But on Sunday it was discovered that one important detail had been forgotten.

At a quarter after nine, James Pearl, the deacon in charge of Sunday school, made his morning rounds. Peeking in on each of the classes, he discovered seven well-scrubbed five-year-olds perched on little wooden chairs around their classroom's table, but no teacher.

"Hi, boys and girls," James said. "Where's your teacher?"

"We don't know."

"Did she go to the supply room for something? Crayons or glue?"

"We don't know."

Suddenly it hit him: Cherry was the missing teacher! Why, Cherry Baker had taught the class for the past six years. How could he have forgotten? More important, what in the world was he going to do now that he had remembered?

"You guys okay? Can you sit tight for just another minute? I'll be right back," he assured the little ones.

Luckily the children didn't require any lengthy talks or explanations. Plied with cookies and apple juice, all seven seemed content to color pictures of Noah and the ark under the eyes of a hastily recruited substitute. They were contentedly coloring when their parents arrived to pick them up.

After a trip to the bathroom and a drink from the fountain, Justin, one of Miz Cherry's five-year-olds, settled into a pew next to his mom, ready to be quiet during the grown-up's worship service. But before things got started, he proudly showed her his picture, the one he'd colored during Sunday school. When Justin held up his picture, he dropped his quarter, the one his mother had given him that morning to put in the Sunday school collection basket.

"Justin," she asked, "is that the money I gave you to give to Jesus?"

"Uh-huh."

"But you still have it."

"Uh-huh."

"Why didn't you give it to Jesus?"

"I couldn't."

"What do you mean, you couldn't?"

"Her wasn't there," he shrugged.

"Who?"

"Jesus. Her wasn't there."

Some adults might smile at Justin's mistake. After all, he's just a little boy. But you can't fool kids; they know what they see. And there is no doubt. Every Sunday, when Justin saw Miz Cherry, he saw Jesus in the flesh.

He's not the only one.

*Let your light so shine before men, that they may see your good works, and glorify your Father which is in heaven.*

MATTHEW 5:16 KJV

TWENTY-THREE

# The Christmas Bike

Thirty-seven-year-old Austin Abercrombie died on a Friday afternoon. He was leaning against a shade tree, enjoying the crisp fall breeze when a rotten, rain-soaked limb cracked, split from the trunk, and hit him square on the back of the head. Eyewitnesses to the event reported that he died instantly.

When all was said and done, Austin's life insurance policy covered funeral expenses but not much more. His boss called to offer condolences to Kitty and the kids, bringing with him a check for two hundred dollars, collected in part from Austin's coworkers. "I know it's not much, ma'am, especially considering you've got another baby on the way, but it's all they could do. I chipped in almost half of this myself," he said.

Employees at the Piggly Wiggly, Fred's Fina gas station, and the Tip Top Barber Shop set out collection jars for Austin's widow ("Bless her heart, she's in the family way, you know") and his five kids. Sympathetic customers dropped in pennies, nickels, dimes, and quarters, even a few dollar bills—whatever they had left after paying their bills. Kitty was touched, and grateful for the help. But the reality was that the funds would not last long. Sitting at the kitchen table, one week after her husband's death, she took stock.

The house, which had belonged to Austin's great-granddaddy, had been willed to Austin a dozen years ago, so there'd be no need to move.

That was good.

Austin had worked all summer getting enough wood to keep a fire going in the house all winter; at least they'd stay warm.

That was good, too.

Kitty would sell the pickup truck and get a bit of cash for it, because she couldn't drive. (Right after they got married, Austin had set out, with great manly confidence, to teach his bride to steer. "Come on, sugar. Hop on in. Ain't nothin' to it." It was not until Kitty got flustered and ran into a tree three times that he made her promise that she would not drive again. "Kit," he explained kindly, "some folks just ain't meant to drive; no shame in that a'tall.")

Lack of transportation would not be a problem, however, since Kitty's house sat near the edge of town. Most anywhere she would need or want to go—school, church, the downtown shops—was within walking distance.

Although these things were in her favor, Kitty had to face the fact that she must find work. Sam and Adam, nine-year-old twins, had already reached that hollow-legged stage where they were hungry all of the time. Molly, eight, was outgrowing all her clothes. Jill, five, and Brady, four, were still at home and underfoot. Working somewhere in town, Kitty realized, would be difficult with the two of them in tow, not to mention when the new baby arrived.

So Kitty started taking in ironing. It was hot and tedious work as she stood hour after hour in the kitchen, pressing other families' nice, new clothes. But it was bearable because Jill stayed in the kitchen with her, chattering away, sprinkling and smoothing, hanging and buttoning.

Known to be a good cook, Kitty began to bake for the public. Tuesdays and Fridays, as soon as they arrived home from school, Adam and Sam set out to deliver their mother's famous custard pies and chocolate layer cakes to housewives around town who favored the taste and quality of Kitty's baked goods. Unable to carry more than one pie or one cake at a time, they sometimes made half a dozen trips back and forth on baking day.

Ironing and dessert making brought in some cash, but it was mostly her Avon sales that kept Kitty and her family afloat. She went door to door, taking Jill and Brady with her, peddling creams and lotions, colors and potions. It wasn't so bad. Folks were nice and most ordered something every time she called. When Kitty's Avon order came in at the post office, Jill and Brady helped her tote it home, unpack it, sort it out, and bag up each customer's products. Sometimes Kitty let Jill try a lipstick sample, and Brady too, except that his brothers teased him when they got home.

As Kitty's belly grew larger, her back began to ache and her feet to swell. "Here, Mama, sit down," the children would urge. "Want some tea, Mama? A piece of cake?" On most days, by the time Kitty, Jill, and Brady arrived home from their Avon rounds, the older children would have prepared the evening meal.

Once dinner was finished and the kitchen was cleaned up, Kitty would limp to the living room, settle into a rocker, and read to the children. They took turns picking what book to read. The boys favored Tarzan novels, the girls something by Zane Gray.

As the time drew near for the birth of her sixth child, Kitty wondered how the children would take to another little brother or sister. She worried a bit about all the time and attention she'd have to devote and hoped that the little ones, especially, would understand.

She needn't have fretted. Once the new baby arrived, Sam, Adam, Molly, Jill, and even Brady thought that he was the most amazing creature they'd ever laid eyes on.

"Look at his little tiny hands," they said wonderingly as they crowded around him.

"Does he have any teeth?"

"Can he see us?"

Kitty christened him Austin, but he was rarely called that. It's a wonder that Kitty's last child ever learned his name, because the children, and even Kitty, got into the habit of calling him The Baby.

"I get to hold The Baby next."

"Mama, The Baby's crying. I think he needs a new diaper."

"Can I help you give The Baby his bath?"

"Brady, can you watch The Baby while I pick the garden?"

The Baby was a plump, good-natured little guy, one of those portable tots who rarely cry, who sleep easily anywhere, and who convey the message that whatever goes on is all right by them. His easygoing temperament was a good thing, because from infancy his brothers and sisters wagged him around on their hips, danced with him, sang to him, and played with him like he was a toy. The girls dressed him up, sometimes in bonnets and hair bows, and the boys enticed him with their toy trucks, making motor sounds as they zoomed the trucks around and around his crib.

When he grew a little older, the children gave The Baby wild piggyback rides, played games with him, and read him stories from their schoolbooks. They loved him and doted on him and couldn't bear for Kitty to spank him. When he did something worthy of a spanking, one of them would scoop him up while another one took the fall.

"No ma'am. The Baby didn't do it, Mama. I did. Really."

When The Baby was six years old, fifteen-year-old Sam noticed that when the two of them walked past Drake's Hardware on their way to the grocery store, The Baby's stride slowed almost to a crawl.

"Whatcha lookin' at?"

"Nothin'. Just nothin'." He would not say more.

Finally, after about the tenth snail's-paced trek, Sam figured it out. Showcased in the window of the hardware store, resplendent in red-painted glory, was a Radio Flyer bicycle. It was a thing of beauty if ever there was one.

That night while The Baby was in the bath, Sam told his family about what he'd seen. "Christmas is coming. Let's get that bike for The Baby."

Their ears perked up. "A bike? For The Baby?"

"Wow! The Baby would love a bike."

"Could we, Mama? Could we *please* get it for him?"

"A bicycle? Sweethearts, there's just no way." Every year, Kitty barely scraped up enough extra cash to purchase small gifts and candy for each of her six. An extravagant gift like a bike—well, she would never have enough. "Besides," she spoke gently, "none of *you* ever got a bike."

They didn't care. They wanted The Baby to have a bike. He would be so surprised!

"What if I got an after-school job? I could help earn the money for it."

"Me too!"

"I can baby-sit."

"I've already got three quarters."

Their mother hesitated. "It's only six weeks until Christmas."

"We can do it."

"Mama, we really, *really* want The Baby to have that bike."

Like an industrious family of squirrels storing away nuts, the five of them set out, determined to get The Baby that bike. Sam talked Eddie at the Tip Top Barber Shop into letting him work on Saturdays, sweeping up. Adam got a paper route. Molly baby-sat every Friday and Saturday night. After school, Jill and Brady pulled weeds for fifty cents an hour, then scoured the roadside for returnable glass soda bottles. Whatever they found, they turned in to the grocery store for three cents each.

Every Saturday night, while The Baby was taking his bath, they emptied out the bike-fund coffee can to see how their funds were adding up.

"How much do we have now?"

"How much more do we need?"

"How many weeks do we have left?"

It was going to be close.

Three weeks before Christmas, Sam picked up extra work on Wednesday and Thursday nights, stocking and cleaning up at the grocery store. Molly skipped lunch. Brady sold his rock collection, Jill her necklace of pink and silver beads.

On the Saturday before Christmas, they discovered that they actually had saved enough—were two dollars over to be exact. Triumphantly the five of them strutted down to Drake's and paid for the bike in cash.

"Wow."

"It's a beauty."

"The Baby is going to love it."

"Will he know how to ride it?"

"Sure he will. He rides his friend Joe's bike all the time."

So as not to get the tires scuffed or dirty, the five of them carried the bike the mile and a half home. Then they hid it under an old quilt in the shed out back.

"He better not find it!"

"Don't worry. He won't."

The next morning the children woke each other up before dawn.

"Brady, get up!"

"Sam! Jill! It's Christmas."

"Mama? You up?"

"Where's The Baby?"

Mama let them all have coffee and play the radio really loud. Their stockings had been filled by Santa with candy, nuts, and some fruit. Mama had two brightly wrapped gifts under the tree for each of them. She passed them out with pride. Sweaters. A puzzle. Water guns and a pocket knife.

"Thank you, Mama."

"I love it, Mama."

Finally it was time. "Brrr. It's cold in here." Molly's complaint was prearranged. "Let's build up the fire."

Sam poked at the flames. "Needs more wood. Can somebody bring some in?"

Sure. The Baby would.

They held their breath as he stepped toward the door, and crept behind him so they could see. The Baby stepped out onto the porch. The Baby stopped. The Baby could not believe his eyes.

"Wow!" he yelped. "Look at this! Who is this for? Come see! Come see!"

His dream had come true.

Sam, Adam, Molly, Jill, Brady, and Austin (at age thirty-one, he sort of likes to be called by his name) had all left to attend colleges and trade schools but one by one have moved back and settled their families in the little town where they grew up. They all have good jobs and they look after their mother.

It's been many years since Kitty took in ironing. She no longer sells Avon, and the cakes and pies she makes are for her own Sunday dinners. Life is good. Her brood of six sees to it.

Molly, who's an old friend of mine, sits at my kitchen table with a cup of hot cocoa. It's early December and we're discussing our gift lists, recipes, and wreaths for our doors. Suddenly, out of the blue, Molly starts talking about that long-ago Christmas as if it happened last year. She describes in great detail the smell of the old house, the taste of the warm, sweetened coffee they drank, the predictably lumpy feel of her stocking.

I've heard this story before, but I listen again. Soon she will get to the part I like to hear best: Molly is standing on the porch with her brothers and sisters, their breath frosty, their teeth chattering. They are laughing, cheering, hopping from one frozen foot to the other, watching The Baby ride his new bike.

Molly giggles as she recalls the way they all took a turn on the bicycle. Even Mama rode, nightgown flapping, hair curlers dropping like a trail of breadcrumbs as she wobbled down the road. She remembers how The Baby rode his Christmas bike all day, how Mama had to threaten him three times to come in once it got dark, and how he talked her into letting him park it inside.

Soon Molly finishes her cocoa, pulls on her sweater, and stands up to go home. "We surprised him all right. He really loved that bike."

As I picture the scene, it occurs to me that at the time, they were all mere children, even Sam and Adam, worthy of bikes themselves. It seems unfair that while they got sweaters, their little brother got a bike.

Molly pauses, her hand on the door.

Perhaps she has read my mind.

"You know, Annette, it wasn't just The Baby's dream that came true that year. It was all of ours."

And from the twinkle in her eye, I can see that it's so.

*Every good and perfect gift is from above, coming down from the Father of the heavenly lights.*

JAMES 1:17

# TWENTY-FOUR

# A Normal Family

Three-year-old Lily's mommy drew her close. Her daddy sat nearby. Oscar, Lily's calico kitty, purred on her lap.

"Honey, we have a special surprise for you."

"You do?" Lily wondered what it might be. A new toy? Maybe ice cream for supper? A visit from Grandma?

No. None of those.

Christmas? Already?

No. Not for another four months, anyway.

It was Mommy who spoke first. "Sweetheart, Daddy and I love having a little girl like you so much that we have decided to get another baby for our family."

"A little baby brother or sister for you to play with," Daddy explained.

"How does that sound, Lily?"

Lily thought it sounded like fun.

When Mommy went to JCPenney to shop for things for the new baby, she took Lily with her. They didn't have to buy a new crib, because the baby would sleep in Lily's old one. But they picked out toys and a mobile to hang over the crib. Mommy asked Lily if she liked the blanket with Winnie the Pooh or the one with clouds on it better. Lily picked the one with Winnie the Pooh. After they finished shopping, the two of them ate burritos at Taco Bell.

Daddy took the computer and his books out of the room where the new baby would sleep. Mommy sewed new curtains for the windows; they had lots of ruffles, balloons, stars, and pretty ribbon ties. Lily helped Mommy take everything out of the closet to make room for the new baby's things.

A nice man with a loud machine came and cleaned all the carpets in the house. "Babies crawl around on the floor a lot," Lily's mom explained. The carpet man gave Lily watermelon bubble gum when he left.

One day when she woke up from her nap, Lily found lots of new things in her room. Her toy box was moved to a different spot. In its place was a little doll crib and a new doll that looked like a real baby, with diapers, blankets, bottles, and clothes. There was even a little diaper bag, like the one Mommy planned to use when the new baby came.

"My goodness, Lily. You have a new baby," Mommy said. "What will you name her?"

Augie sounded good.

"Augie," repeated Mommy. "You're going to name the baby *Augie?*"

She was.

"Augie?" asked Daddy when he got home from work.

"Augie," repeated Lily.

Mommy and Daddy agreed that Augie was a fine name for a baby.

That night, Mommy showed Lily how to bathe Augie in the sink, how to dry her off, and how to dress her in a diaper and pajamas.

"Night-night, Augie," Lily said when she put her new baby to bed. "Don't cry."

Lily's Mommy got very fat. She got so fat that her green robe would not button anymore. Mommy was surprised when she found out from the doctor that there was more than one baby in her tummy. She was very surprised when she learned that *four* babies would be coming to live at their house.

Aunt Teresa came to visit for a while so Mommy could stay in bed. Aunt Teresa, Lily, and Mommy had picnics on top of the covers. They played games like Old Maid and Go Fish. They looked at pictures and watched lots of movies. Aunt Teresa swept and mopped, washed Lily's clothes, and made her grilled cheese. She took Lily with her to the store and let her pick out which kind of cereal Mommy liked best.

"Apple Jacks or Rice Krispies?" Aunt Teresa asked.

"Cap'n Crunch," assured Lily.

When the babies were born, Daddy and Aunt Teresa took Lily to the hospital to see Mommy. She was much skinnier now. She could button her green robe. Lily brought her mommy flowers and a picture she had colored at home. She sat in bed with Mommy and ate the apple pie that came with her lunch.

Mommy came home in three days, but the babies still lived at the hospital. She and Daddy went to see the babies every day, but Lily did not get to go. She had to wait many days to see the new babies. They were sleeping, always sleeping.

When Lily finally did get to look in a big window and see them, she thought that the babies were very, very red. That afternoon she went with Daddy to Wal-Mart, where he bought another crib. Daddy said that for a while two babies could sleep together. When they got bigger they would each get their own bed. Daddy also bought bags and bags of diapers, and some bottles, too.

Lots and lots of friends came to see Mommy and Daddy and Lily. They brought food, like meat loaf and banana pudding, and presents for the babies, like clothes and toys and blankets. Everyone kept asking when the babies were going to come home. Mommy told them soon. Really, really soon.

One day Aunt Teresa stayed with Lily while Mommy and Daddy went to get some of the babies—two boy babies and a girl. The last one, another boy baby, had to stay in the hospital for a little while longer.

Lily stood at the window and watched for them to come back. Finally she saw the car pull into the drive. It took Mommy and Daddy a long time to get the babies out of their car seats, but finally they brought them in, all wrapped up in blankets. Everybody was talking, two of the babies were crying, and even the telephone was ringing.

"Let's get them settled and into bed," Mommy told Daddy. "This one needs a diaper change and that one is spitting up."

Aunt Teresa held Lily. She could not go into the babies' room today because she had a runny nose and might make the babies sick. She could see them tomorrow. Mommy might even let her hold a baby if she washed her hands. Aunt Teresa was sorry, but for now, Lily couldn't go any closer than the doorway of the babies' room. This was a big disappointment. Lily wanted to touch the babies. She needed to see if they had any teeth. It was hard to wait.

After a while the other baby came home. Mommy and Daddy were very happy, but four babies were a lot of work. Somebody, either Aunt Teresa, Grandma, or someone from church, came every day to help. There was always a baby to change, a baby to feed, a baby to bathe, rock, burp, or dress.

Once she got over her runny nose, Lily got to sit next to Mommy or Daddy on the couch and hold a baby anytime she wanted. Sometimes she got to hold a bottle for a baby. She was a big help all day long. If a baby spit up, Lily would go and get a rag. If a baby needed a diaper, she would get that, too.

She was a very good big sister.

Lily's Mom and Dad, Jan and Eddie, loved her very much, but they were concerned. They knew that suddenly being thrust into role of big sister for quadruplets had to be terribly difficult for her. For four years running, Lily had been the center of their attention, the one member of the family that both friends and strangers had stopped to admire. It hurt them to see that Lily literally got stepped on in the stampede of folks eager to see the new babies. Few people were sensitive to what their oldest daughter must feel.

Eddie looked up sibling rivalry on the internet. Some children, he learned, were so hostile toward their younger siblings that rage built up inside them. They might even try to hurt a new baby in the house.

But Lily handled the babies gently and did not try to take away their toys. She did not seem to feel rage, but perhaps she was just hiding it well.

Jan talked to Lily's pediatrician about her concerns. "She's so young herself and she's used to being the baby. I'm afraid she's going to feel left out."

Taking the doctor's advice, Jan began spending two afternoons a week alone with Lily. It was a tremendous sacrifice to hire baby-sitters for the quads, but Jan felt it was worth spending any amount of money to give Lily the attention she needed. On their afternoons out, she took Lily shopping, to the zoo, or to the children's museum. Sometimes they ate ice cream and sometimes they went to the park.

Lily's response to her mother's efforts was not what Jan expected. "When will the babies be big enough to come with us, Mommy?" Lily asked every week. "What if the baby-sitter has to go home soon?" she worried. "Do the babies miss us?"

One Sunday when the quads were six months old, Lily got to go to church with just her mom and dad. On that particular day, Jan and Eddie decided to leave the babies at home with Aunt Teresa. It was a nasty, rainy day—not a good one to take little ones outside. Plus it would give the two of them the chance to pay special attention to Lily.

Lily loved church. She enjoyed looking at the stained-glass windows and listening to the music of the organ. Rather than going to children's church, she chose to stay in the sanctuary, to sit on Daddy's lap and help him hold the hymnbook. When a tall man prayed, she sat very still, and when the sermon started, she cuddled next to Mommy with her Jesus' Friends coloring book.

Once the sermon was over, the minister of the church called for a young couple to come down to the front. They stood before the congregation, shyly eager to have their new little baby blessed and dedicated to the Lord. When it was done, the whole congregation clapped. The baby, named John Allen, slept through the whole thing.

But Lily didn't miss a thing. She sat up on her knees on the pew to get a good look. Just last week Mommy and Daddy had brought all four of the babies for their dedications. Daddy had held a baby, Mommy had held a baby, Grandma had held a baby, and Aunt Teresa had held a baby. During the middle of the dedication, one of the babies started to cry. Blessing four babies took quite a while, and before it was over, all of them were crying.

On the way home from church, Mommy talked to her about what the dedication of baby John Allen meant. It was a promise from everyone in the church that they would love the baby, pray for the baby, and help the mommy and daddy to raise the baby the way that God would want them to. Did Lily understand? Did she have any questions?

She did have one.

"Okay, honey, what is it?"

"Where," Lily asked with much concern, "are the *rest* of the mommy and daddy's babies? Did they leave them at home?"

*Children are a gift from God; they are his reward.*

PSALM 127:3 TLB

# TWENTY-FIVE

# Road Show

Southern men are among the most mannerly males that today's modern woman can expect to encounter. Doubt my words, ladies? Try this experiment: Next time you find yourself in my neck of the woods, stop in at the post office. Be sure it's morning—say around 10:00. The place will be busy, because we rural residents must collect our daily mail from individual post-office boxes since we lack home delivery. Midmorning is the time our postmaster strives to have the mail in our boxes, so lots of folks show up about then.

Pull your car into one of the half-dozen parking lot spots, get out, and approach the post-office door. Plan to open it yourself.

Go on. Give it a try.

Didn't happen, did it?

It's a fact. No matter how quick you're moving, or how far he's standing from the door, a good Southern man is *not* going to allow a lady to open that door for herself. I know. . . . I know. . . . You're twenty-two and you run three miles a day. He's ninety-six, uses a walker, and has his oxygen tank in the car. That does not matter; it has nothing to do with it. No matter how loudly you protest, there is no way that you, little lady, are going to open that big, heavy door for yourself. That just wouldn't be polite.

Along with their good manners, Southern men have lots of other appealing attributes. Most of them know how to cook, almost all of them love babies, and without exception they respect elderly ladies. Now tell me—what more could a woman ask for in a man?

It's not just grilling a tender steak that Southern men can do. They cook great, chill-chasing chilies, tender beef stews, and the best scrambled eggs you'll ever put in your mouth. It is said that the way to a man's heart is through his stomach, but I'm here to tell you that, judging by the contented wives and mothers I know, the same holds true for women.

Now about those babies and elderly ladies. Southern men know how to charm both.

Every Southern male I know loves babies. Unafraid of even the tiniest newborn, men scoop them from their mothers' arms, pick them up, play with them in church, and tickle them under their arms. At community gatherings even teenage boys are likely to be seen casually carting around a baby—often a toddler cousin or their older sister's youngest kid.

True confession? There is just something about a big, rough-and-tumble fellow playing peekaboo with a soft little baby that melts the hearts of us Southern gals. My daughter, Rachel, who's sixteen, confides that if the guys her age knew how the sight of them playing with a baby makes a girl's heart turn to mush, they'd beg, buy, or borrow one to have for the effect.

Traditionally we Southern women have let our men run (or at least think they run) lots of things. But truth be told, in many of our families it is an elderly woman who's really in charge. We know it. She knows it. We wouldn't have it any other way.

Whether she's our mother, our grandmother, our god-mother, or even someone else's relative, if she's old and she's female, we treat her with the dignity and respect she's earned. Male members of the family treat elderly ladies with special regard. In her presence, they remove their hats and, depending on the color of her carpet, maybe their shoes or boots before they go in her house. They hug her neck when they see her, and they don't fail to address her with a "yes, ma'am."

These Southern guys bring the family matriarch bath powder on her birthday and have double orchid corsages delivered to her house on Mother's Day. If she's an elderly woman and she wants to go to Sunday school and church, they take her. Should she hanker for a pack of Double Mint gum—well, they go to the drugstore and get it for her. If she's hot, they turn up the air conditioner. If she's cold, they stoke the flames in the fireplace.

What an elderly Southern lady wants, an elderly Southern lady gets.

Granted, even the best of the guys may gripe and carry on when they leave her house, but none, not even one of them, would disrespect her to her face. It just wouldn't be right.

Perhaps after hearing about all these admirable traits, you have concluded that Southern men are perfect and totally without flaw.

Girls, don't we wish that were true!

For along with the failings common to all males of the species (watching sports all the time, failing to ask for directions—you know the rest), Southern men have some quirks that are unique to them.

We Southern women expect that our men will bring anything into the house. Depending on our man's profession, on any given day we may come home to find a sick baby calf, a broken-down lawn mower, or part of a power transmission in the middle of our kitchen floor. If we are really lucky, our man will have first laid down one of our good, company towels. While a normal man's home may be his castle, a Southern man's home is where he brings in stuff that, seeing as how the weather is about to turn bad, simply ought not to be left outside.

Other imperfections peculiar to Southern men? Let's see. When preparing a meal for one of these guys, a woman should keep in mind the four basic food groups of the South: You have your grilled steak, your chicken-fried steak, your chopped steak, and your catfish. Should a meal set before a Southern man not contain any of these foods, it will be looked upon with great sorrow and scorn. Southern men do not appreciate what they deem "lady food." This tends to take the fun out of trying new recipes.

But the most unpleasant Southern male characteristic of all is the penchant they have for two particularly vile forms of tobacco. I speak not of cigarettes or cigars, although some of our men do indeed light up, but of the type of tobacco that comes in a foil pouch or a can. In powdered form, the stuff's called snuff, and a person who uses it is said to take a dip. When it looks like moist brown leaves, the product is called chewing tobacco, and logically it is designed to be chewed. That doesn't sound so bad, you may think—no smoke, no ashes, no burns on the clothing. Think again. Both snuff and chewing tobacco require that during their use a man must expectorate—*spit*—copious amounts of nasty brown liquid into a cup or a can.

Which, yes, is every bit as bad as it sounds.

Folks know by now that cigarettes are bad for one's health. What about this kind of tobacco? Is it bad, too? You bet. Both products have been linked to irritations and malignancies of both the tongue and the gums. Do users of such know that the stuff's bad for them? Sure they do. That's why lots of them have tried to quit in recent years.

Although I can gladly report that my dad managed to give it up many years ago, when I was growing up, he loved his chewing tobacco. He kept a wad of the stuff in his jaw almost all the time, and I remember that he kept a spit cup next to his chair as well as one in his truck. Not once, as far as I know, did he spill the vile contents of either of those cups— a fact that amazes me to this day.

Dad's favorite brand of chewing tobacco went by the pleasant-sounding name of Beech Nut. He bought half a dozen red-and-white-striped bags at a time, at either the feed store in town or at the Texaco station where he pumped his gas. So that he'd have it when he needed it, Dad kept pouches of Beech Nut in the house, in the barn, in his truck, and in the glove compartment of my mother's car.

Although the small town where I live is considered very safe, there are a few things that a careful mother these days would never do. No mother I know would leave a child alone in a parked car for even a moment while she runs into the grocery store or the dry cleaners. However, in my mother's day no one gave a second thought to doing such a thing.

On this particular spring day, my little brothers, twins, are three years old. While the two of them look nothing alike, they are close in size, have big blue eyes, and are two of the cutest little things that you have ever seen. Because this is Tuesday, errand day, they are with my mother in her new Plymouth station wagon. The plan is for the three of them to go to the grocery store, the hardware store, the bakery, and the bank. So far, they've made the first three of their stops. At each place of business my mother takes the boys in. They are cute, and she enjoys showing them off, but doing so wears her out because she cannot take her eyes off of them for a minute, lest they get themselves into something they shouldn't.

By now it is close to noon, and the boys are getting tired and cranky. My mother is weary, too. Since her business at the bank will only take a minute, she decides to leave the boys in the car while she goes inside. The bank building faces the town square, and she'll park right close to the door. Once she's found a parking spot—not in front of the bank as she'd hoped, but still only two stores down—my mother rolls the windows down low enough for the boys to get air, but not so low that they can fall out. She figures to be gone less than five minutes, ten at the most.

"Back in a minute, okay, boys? Sit right here." She gives them each a graham cracker from her purse.

My mother dashes into the bank, fully prepared to make her deposit, get her cash, and sprint back to the car. She has not planned on two of the tellers being sick or on having to stand in a long line. Should she leave? Come back later? Go out to the car and bring my brothers in? Not wanting to lose her place in line, my mother decides to wait. Besides, by now both boys will be covered with graham-cracker crumbs, and the line seems to be moving pretty fast.

When she exits the bank with cash, coins, and deposit receipt in hand, my mother spots the crowd gathered around her car. Folks are standing three deep, peering into the windows on both sides. No! Something must be wrong! Her heart races, and she sprints toward the scene.

But then my mother's panic turns to dread when she realizes that folks in the crowd are laughing, pointing, and slapping their knees. "Excuse me. Excuse me." She tries to part the crowd. "Please excuse me. Can I get through?" Observers are having such a good time that it is difficult to make herself heard.

Finally my mother makes it to the driver's-side door and gets a good look. Her boys are still in the car. That is good. They are not sick or hurt. That is good, too.

Nothing else is good.

They are buck naked, both of them; they have pulled off every stitch of their clothing. What's more, the twins have helped themselves to my dad's chewing tobacco, and it tastes pretty good. Standing up in the front seat, each of them holds a bag in their hands. Their cheeks are packed tight, the stuff hangs from their mouths, and from their fat tummies to their toes, they are covered with sticky brown goo.

My mother wants to crawl between the cracks in the sidewalk.

"Mommy! Mommy!" they squeal when they see her.

"Mrs. Woodall? That you?" Members of the small-town crowd recognize her now. This only adds to their fun.

"Couple of fine boys you've got there!" Chuckles ripple through the crowd.

"Take after their daddy, don't they?" Folks hoot with laughter and slap at their knees.

My mother smiles weakly, opens the car door, and tells the boys to scoot over.

"Can we get out now?" one of them asks.

"No. We have to go home."

"But I need to go potty!"

The crowd goes wild.

My twin brothers are all grown up now. Being good traditional Southern men, both of them know their manners, both can cook, and both of them are at their best around babies and elderly ladies.

They have, however, broken with one long-held male Southern tradition. As far as I know, in the past thirty-five years or so, neither of them has smoked, dipped, or chewed.

Perhaps once was enough.

I know it was for my mom!

> *May your father and mother be glad;*
> *may she who gave you birth rejoice!*
>
> PROVERBS 23:25

# TWENTY SIX

# A Perfect Friend

When my daughter, Rachel, was five years old, she spent many an hour perched on a faded lawn chair she'd dragged from the garage and set up by the concrete curb that ran in front of our house. Sitting in that chair, she would look up and down our quiet street, turning her head from side to side—often for twenty minutes or more at a time.

*What,* I wondered the first time I saw her from my kitchen window, *is my little girl doing?* It was obvious she was watching for something or someone—but what? Who? When I went outside to ask, she nonchalantly informed me that she was waiting.

"Waiting?"

"For my friends."

Of course. Being the youngest child on the block, Rachel was the only neighborhood kid who didn't get to go to school every day.

"But honey, school won't be out for another two hours. You're going to get tired of sitting out here. Come on in and you can help me bake cookies."

"Not *those* friends," she explained. "Chew. Aunt Lisa."

I was confused.

"Here they come now." Then, so that I wouldn't embarrass myself, she whispered, "You can't see them, Mommy. Wait here."

Now I understood. These were imaginary friends—Rachel's first.

I smiled and watched as she slid from her chair and trotted down the driveway. From the way she was talking with her hands, it was apparent that Rachel was engaged in an important conversation with, I presumed, the two imaginary friends. But then I saw the expression on her face turn serious.

It seemed that there had been a mistake. Chew was not here after all. According to Aunt Lisa, Chew was in the hospital.

"Poor thing," I sympathized. "What happened to her?"

"Well," Rachel said, placing her hands on her hips, "Chew climbed up on the roof of her house, fell down, and broke her head off."

Oh, my! I stood there awkwardly, not sure how one behaved in the face of such news.

"But she's coming home tonight after supper."

What a relief!

"Aunt Lisa and I are going to have tea now. Bye, Mommy."

Unmistakably dismissed, I walked back into the house to finish washing my dishes.

After that first introduction, our family came to expect frequent visits from both Chew and Aunt Lisa. Sometimes the pair showed up for lunch, and we set them a place. (Aunt Lisa liked water; Chew always had milk.) Occasionally the two of them went on trips with us and sat buckled in next to each other, squeezed into the back seat between Rachel and her big brother.

Both of Rachel's new friends were extremely well-behaved guests, but obviously, poor Chew had lots of problems. At least a dozen times Rachel sadly reported to me that Chew was, once again, in the hospital.

Why? What happened?

The news was almost always the same: Chew had climbed up on a roof, fallen off, and broken something. She was in the hospital, but would come home in a day or two. Sometimes we made Get Well cards for Chew. Occasionally Rachel would go visit Chew in the hospital and come back and give me a report. Chew's treatment, according to Rachel, inevitably involved a lot of Band-Aids and Sprite.

Rachel is now sixteen years old. Last week while we were folding clothes on my bed, we reminisced about some of the fun times we'd had when she was a little girl.

"Do you remember Chew and Aunt Lisa, your imaginary friends?" I asked. "They stopped coming around when you started to school."

"Of course."

"Poor Chew," I joked, "she was always getting hurt. But then again, she always got better."

Rachel smiled at the memory.

"Kids have imaginary playmates for lots of reasons," I knowingly observed. "Chew must have helped you deal with secret fears about accidents and such." (I have, it should be noted, taken *several* college-level psychology courses.)

Rachel looked at me kind of funny.

"Well, why else did Chew keep falling off of the house?" My voice was, I admit, a tiny bit smug.

"Mom," Rachel explained in that don't-you-know-anything voice that teenagers do so well, "I wasn't scared of anything back then. Chew's daddy was a roofer. She was always falling off the tops of houses because she was up there helping him!"

Why, I hadn't known. "You mean all those times she was up on a roof . . ."

"Handing him nails," Rachel said, finishing my thought. "Chew was a very helpful child."

"Of course."

"She's sitting right there, you know."

"Rachel!"

"Really, Mom. She is. Oh, Mom, you just stepped on Chew!"

Giggling, I threw a pillow at my sassy child's head.

None of the grown-ups I know have imaginary friends. But wouldn't it be fun if all of us did? The way I have it figured, if we had an imaginary friend, she would call us when we are lonely and bring us casseroles when we are busy. She would inform us when we have lipstick on our teeth and would notice when we've lost a whole three-quarters of a pound. She would always want to see the movies we want to see, and when we decide to share a single entrée before splurging on individual desserts, she would never, ever, try to talk us into the baked fish.

She would, in short, be the perfect friend.

Know anyone like her? Me neither. The friends I have are too much like me—flawed. They have faults, they mess up, they get tangled up, and they do all kinds of things wrong.

But I'm so glad! Most of us, in spite of our faults, are truly doing the best we can. Flawed people like you and me are what make life interesting, after all. I can't think of anyone with whom I'd rather share a piece of pie and a mug of cold milk.

Can you?

*You who dwell in the gardens*
*with friends in attendance,*
*let me hear your voice!*

Song of Songs 8:13

**Annette Smith,** a registered nurse, speaker, and writer, is married to her college sweetheart, Randy, and is the mother of almost-grown children Russell and Rachel. Much of the material in this book Annette gleaned from her family and from more than two decades spent observing the antics of her small-town neighbors and friends.

Annette loves to receive comments from her readers. If you wish to contact her, please write to Annette Smith in care of Baker Book House.

For information on scheduling Annette to speak at your next event, please contact:

Speak Up Speaker Services
(888) 870-7719